THE FOG PRINCES

THE FOG PRINCES

FLORENCE WARDEN

Originally published in 1889.

Published by Wildside Press.
Visit us online at wildsidepress.com.

CHAPTER I.

AMONG the noblemen's seats of the United Kingdom there are many more imposing, many more ancient, than Llancader Castle; but there are none better adapted to the requirements of modern life, none where lifts and electric bells combine more harmoniously with old tapestry and heavily decorated ceilings. It is built in the hybrid classical style of the Jacobean period, and is pleasantly placed among lawns and trees and artificial fishponds not far from the banks of the River Wye.

The Earl of St. Austell, by far the largest landowner in this part of the country, and possessor of estates rich in relics of the past, knew how to avail himself of all the resources of the present. He had the reputation in the country of being a good and beneficent landlord; while in town, in the greenrooms of theatres where ballet was the principal attraction, he had a reputation for munificence of quite another sort.

Lady St. Austell was an amiable and still handsome woman, easy-going to a fault, whose chief grief and grievance was, not her husband's peccadilloes, but the fact that she had not borne him an heir. In their three daughters the earl took but slight interest; and the countess being allowed full liberty to conduct their education on what principles she pleased, tried to make up for their not being sons by giving them the same education as if they had been.

If these young ladies had possessed brains or strength of character out of the common, this system might have answered very well. Unluckily, however, they were commonplace girls, and their unusual training only served to foster a belief in their own superiority, and thus to emphasize a certain lack of feminine grace and charms which, considering their parentage, was difficult to account for.

On a warm afternoon in early August the eldest and the youngest daughter were sitting at work in a pleasant room, pannelled with light oak and hung with large flowered cretonne, which looked out on to a wide lawn dotted with trees and brightened with flower-beds. In the distance could be seen, through a clearing made specially in the thick groves which line the banks of the winding Wye, the rugged grey walls of ruined Carstow Castle.

"Where's Marion?" asked Lady Catherine suddenly, looking up from a Latin exercise she was preparing for her tutor.

Lady Catherine was a reddish-haired, freckled little girl of sixteen, very plump and very merry looking.

"Oh, wherever Rees Pennant is, I suppose," answered her eldest sister, Elizabeth, glancing out of window between the stitches of crewel work over which she was bending.

1

Lady Elizabeth was, like her younger sister, round-cheeked and blue-eyed; she had a fair complexion, golden hair, eyebrows and eye lashes, a self-satisfied expression, and a figure which all the back-boards, reclining boards, and all the dancing masters in Europe could never have saved from being round-shouldered and "dumpy."

Lady Catherine burst into a merry laugh, and from a sofa in the shadier depths of the long room a plaintive, but cracked, voice wailed out a request in French that "miladi Katte" would be quieter, and would remember that "madame la comtesse," her mother, wished her to overcome her propensity to unladylike outbursts of merriment.

Mademoiselle de Laval, the duenna of the earl's daughters, had been specially chosen for the post for her abnormal ugliness, Lord St. Austell holding that women's virtue was always in inverse proportion to their beauty. He had over-reached himself, however, for mademoiselle, being a martyr to neuralgia and rheumatism, and finding herself very comfortable in her Welsh home, would not for worlds have endangered her situation by any indiscreet prying into the amusements of her charges.

Lady Kate, with a grimace in her direction, crossed the room to her sister, and sat down on a footstool by her side, with a scandal-loving expression on her face.

"Rees Pennant," she repeated in a hissing whisper; "do you think she is in love with him?"

"I am sure of it!" cried Elizabeth, with all the superiority in such matters which twenty possesses over sixteen.

Lady Kate chuckled to herself with intense amusement.

"Of course he isn't in love with her," she suggested, with a sister's partiality. "Marion is so gawky and Rees is so handsome. It would be like a figure of Raffaele falling in love with an Anglo-Saxon saint."

"What's the use of their falling in love, either of them?" said Elizabeth prosaically. "They can't marry."

"Why not? He is the eldest son, and Captain Pennant's family is as old as ours. And look at us! We're not beauties, and I know papa does not mean to give us very handsome fortunes, or else you would have had an offer before this. You're twenty, you know."

"Certainly. And I don't want any offer," answered her sister, not without a pardonable suspicion of tartness. "But I certainly shouldn't condescend to flirt with a man beneath me in rank, and without a penny. And there must be madness in the family, or Captain Pennant would never have adopted a fisherman's baby and brought it up as his own child."

"Deborah's very pretty," said Lady Kate, thoughtfully. "If we were half as good-looking we should have been photographed all over the place as beauties."

2

"Pretty! Do you think so?" asked her sister, with an air of matter-of-fact impartiality. "I don't admire those big, coarse-looking women. I like a face which shows signs of the higher intelligence, a face which lights up. And Deborah has no conversation. I can't admire a girl without conversation."

"Papa can though," said Kate, rather maliciously. "He admires Deborah, and I am sure you can't say he likes coarse-looking women."

"A gentlemen's taste in beauty is not the same as a lady's," said Elizabeth, moving restlessly, and wishing that her persistent little sister would let her change this awkward subject.

"I know it isn't. I expect some women would admire Mademoiselle de Laval," whispered Kate, glancing towards the dozing French governess, whose wide nose and mouth, leathern complexion and well-defined moustache formed a combination of feminine attractions rarely to be met with. "But do you know, Betty, after mature consideration of the subject, I would rather be pretty according to the gentlemen's standard than according to the ladies'."

Lady Elizabeth, who, although extremely erudite, was rather dull, did not perceive all the point of this speech, but felt that the pert girl was slyly laughing at her. She was too good-tempered to grow cross, however; she only grew didactic.

"You can't expect much refinement from a fisherman's daughter, of course," she said in obstinate tone. "I've always pitied poor Mrs. Pennant—who comes of one of the oldest families in England, better than her husband's—for having to submit to such an absurd caprice of his. She feels it, poor thing, dreadfully."

"Yes, and turns up her eyes over it, and acts quite a pretty pantomime of resignation over it still, though Deborah's been one of the family eighteen years. The consequence is that the boys have never learnt to look upon her as a sister, and so they're falling in love with her. Godwin, and Hervey—yes, and Rees too, whatever Marion may like to think."

"So much the better. Then Rees can marry the girl, though I think one of the gamekeepers would be a more suitable match."

"Betty, how can you? You talk just like an ordinary spiteful girl. Deborah is as much a lady as we are ourselves."

"Very well then. Don't let's talk any more about it. We shall only quarrel. And all about a girl who thinks that a smattering of French, German and the piano form a good education."

There was a pause. But Kate, who always liked to worry a subject to death, soon broke out again.

"Betty, why do you think papa wouldn't let Rees marry Marion? He's so fond of Rees, he really treats him almost as if he were his own son."

"You don't understand papa," said Elizabeth, with authority. "He always seems so easy-going that people don't guess that he's just like a rock underneath. Nobody thinks so much of class distinctions and money distinctions—those are almost the same thing nowadays—as he does. Rees would have no more chance as a son-in-law than—than Amos Goodhare," she ended contemptuously.

Lady Kate laughed and pretended to shudder.

"Oh, old Amos," she cried with real disgust. "Don't speak of that man. I can't bear him. I think he has such shifting eyes and such a bad, horrible face. I never could understand why papa allowed such a man into the house at all."

"He is really a well-read man, and he looks just such a man as a librarian ought to look," said Elizabeth, in a reserved tone, as if she knew more than she intended to tell.

Kate looked hard at her sister, and then edged her footstool close up to her side.

"Betty," she whispered, with a very curious expression, "did you ever notice the extraordinary likeness there is between Mr. Goodhare and—papa?"

"Nonsense, child," said Lady Elizabeth, blushing violently, and trying to rise.

But Lady Kate, who was a sturdily built girl, with little fat, but muscular hands, held her down.

"Of course, he looks much older, because he doesn't dye his hair and mustache, as papa does, and because he wears a beard. But really, do you know, Betty, I've sometimes thought——"

But here Lady Elizabeth, who was also a robust young woman, disengaged herself, with no great gentleness, from her sister's clasp, and with an almost frightened, "Hush, Kitty, hush; you mustn't let your tongue run on so," left her to form her own opinion on the subject of this sudden closure of the discussion.

Lady Kate mused for some time on this point, until at length it occurred to her to get a peep at Mr. Goodhare by the light of her new suspicions. She knew where he was to be found, for, to do him justice, the librarian loved his books, and appeared to live for nothing else. He had lately been employed in collecting papers and documents and books of reference bearing on the history of Carstow Castle, of which most interesting ruin Lady Marion proposed to compile an exhaustive chronicle.

No subject more fascinating could well have been chosen. The old place, after having suffered many vicissitudes of fortune under Plantagenets and Tudors, had been almost destroyed during the Great Rebellion, when it was held for King Charles by a brave little garrison, who did not surrender until all hope of escape had been cut off by a fearless Puritan soldier. Swimming across the river with a knife in his mouth, he cut adrift the boat on which the defenders of the castle counted for their flight. Some years later a tower of the desolated castle was patched up into a prison for one of the "regicides," who passed there a pleasantly mitigated captivity, and was buried in the churchyard of the quiet little old town.

From these events Lady Marion had determined to construct a strictly impartial chronicle, which should, however, illustrate in a marked manner her own strictly impartial views on the subject of hereditary monarchy and the powers of Parliament. Therefore, Amos Goodhare, the librarian, had been for the past few weeks employed in digging out, from the vast hoards of accumulated records of the past with which not only the library, but various corners of roomy Llancader were filled, such documents as seemed likely to be of use to the young lady in her vast undertaking.

It was among the nooks and crannies of the castle, therefore, that Lady Kate set about her search for the librarian; and it was in one of the dustiest corners of a scarcely used wing of the building that, after a long hunt, she found him.

There was here a little awkward staircase, which led up to a tower, long since given up, for its draughtiness, to the bats and the mice. Underneath this staircase was an oddly-shaped recess, as large as a small room, where, behind some boxes, boards, and similar lumber, a rough chest, full to the top of yellow and musty papers, had that very day been unearthed by the indefatigable librarian. Lady Kate, creeping about the corridors and staircases with careful feet, heard the rustle of papers as soon as she entered the passage in which the tower staircase was. She stopped, listened, advanced on tiptoe until she was close to the outer pile of lumber. She did not at first dare to peep round at Amos Goodhare, for she wanted to get an opportunity of studying his face unseen by him. She knew he was there, though, for whenever Amos found anything which interested him he omitted a series of low grunts of satisfaction. And now he was grunting at a great rate.

Lady Kate, after half choking with suppressed laughter at his curious little cries and murmurs of excitement, decided that he was too deeply interested in something he had discovered to take any notice of her. So, with cautious steps, holding her breath, she crept through the space between the piled-up boxes and the staircase. He could not have been more favorably placed for her proposed inspection. A long lancet window lighted the staircase, and the bottom panes came low enough to illuminate the space below. Standing close under the little patch of dusty glass was the librarian, holding in his hands some large sheets of paper, which Lady

Kate perceived to be old and yellow-looking. He was far too intent upon deciphering the contents of the papers to notice the plump and curious girl's face peering up at him a couple of feet from the floor.

Lady Kate's design of comparing the librarian's face with her father's was forgotten with her first glance at Amos Goodhare, who was a tall, slender, eminently gentlemanly-looking man, with grey hair and beard, grey eyes, which gazed habitually on the ground, and slightly stooping shoulders. For she saw his usually composed features lighted up with excitement so strong that his nostrils were dilated, his breath came fast and his eyes looked fierce, wide open and almost lurid. His long, white hands shook as he clutched at the yellowing papers, or passed his fingers, in feverish restlessness, through his still thick and curly grey hair.

Little Lady Kate's plump face grew white with horror; she thought the librarian had gone mad. Over-devotion to the books had done it, she supposed. At any rate, she was too much frightened to stay and speculate as to the cause of this horrible event. She crept back into the passage on all fours, as she had come, and fled away as softly as she could.

On the floor below she met her sister Marion, who had just come in, and who was, as Kate afterwards described it, "looking sentimental."

Lady Marion was, on the whole, the least attractive of the three sisters. She had not the stolid, but "comfortable," look of the eldest, nor the merry eyes and laughing little pursed-up mouth of the youngest. She was a tall, bony, angular girl, fair, like the others, but without the pink color they had in their cheeks. Her hair was a little darker than theirs, and of an unpleasing length, as it had been cut quite short and then allowed to grow, the result of which was that little ends and tufts stuck out straight in all directions from the tiny little knob she wore at the back of her neck. Her nose was long, her mouth was wide, and her light blue eyes were without fire. Nevertheless there was a certain look, not only of good nature, but of gentleness and affection, in her face, which made her affectation of masculine manners and speech rather pathetic. For Lady Marion had the warmest and deepest nature of the three sisters, therefore it was on her that their anomalous education had worked the most disastrous effects. She was always yearning to show "strength of mind," when, as a matter of fact, the strength her character really possessed did not lie at all in mental attributes, but in the more womanly qualities which she despised.

When her younger sister fell against her, whispering fearsomely, "Oh, Marion, Mr. Goodhare's gone mad!" Lady Marion instantly assumed a manly and devil-may-care front, and said in a deep voice:

"Where is he?"

Whereas, if she had been really a person of much common sense, she would have decided at once that her sister's statement was a wild exaggeration.

Lady Kate briefly described where and how she had found him. Then a happier idea crossed Marion's mind.

"Perhaps he's got hold of something," she mused. "And I believe he's quite capable of keeping back important papers, and bringing out a rival work to mine, compiled from authorities he has kept from me."

For Lady Marion shared the common mistrust of Amos Goodhare, which was, perhaps, only a result of his extreme reserve.

"He looks wickeder than ever, at any rate," murmured Kate, as the sisters went softly up the stairs together.

"Look here," whispered Marion, when they had reached the upper floor, and come in sight of the tower staircase at the other end of a long, dark corridor. "You call him out suddenly, as if something had happened, and I'll watch him on the stairs from the space between the staircase and the window. Then I'll see what he does with the papers, and try to get in and have a look at them."

"All right," whispered Lady Kate.

And they stole along the corridor to the further end.

CHAPTER II.

THE two girls carried out their plan beautifully. Marion crept softly up the tower staircase as far as the window. Then, crouching down, she managed to peep between the dusty panes and the side of the staircase, and saw the top of the librarian's head, which moved from side to side as he scanned the pages of a discolored MS.

Suddenly, ringing down the corridor came a cry in a high, girlish voice, which caused Amos to start and mechanically to hide away under his coat the paper he was reading. Marion noted this action with a suspicious eye.

"Mr. Goodhare, Mr. Goodhare! Where are you? Come! Quick!" the second young conspirator was crying lustily.

"Here I am, your ladyship, at your service," called out the librarian, as the girl's voice sounded nearer and nearer.

At the same moment he opened the old chest he had been ransacking, and thrust the document he had been reading deep down among a mass of other old papers, from which the dust rose in a cloud as his hand moved them. To Lady Marion's delight, he had dropped the last page on the ground. But she had scarcely congratulated herself on the fact when, turning, he perceived the missing leaf, and, not having time to put it into the chest with the rest, dropped it into his pocket. Then he hastened out of his corner to meet the young girl, and addressed her in his usual suave, respectful and dignified manner:

"What can I do for your ladyship?"

"I want you to help me with my Latin exercise. There are some dreadfully hard words in it this time."

"I shall be delighted," said he, as he followed the young girl downstairs.

But in his grave and beautifully modulated voice Lady Marion detected a tone of impatience at the trivial cause of this interruption. She was by this time already in the nook under the stairs, making the most of her time, for she guessed that it would not be long before Amos would find an excuse for returning to the occupation which had absorbed him so deeply. She flung open the chest with violence, which caused its old hinges to creak and little splinters to fly off the worm-eaten wood, while she, half choked by the dust, groped blindly among the mass of mouldering, musty parchments, pamphlets and papers. It was some minutes before the air was clear enough, and her eyes sufficiently used to the obscurity of the ill-lighted corner, for her to begin her search in earnest. Deep down into the withered-looking heap she dived, and, after many a futile plunge, fished up at last a crumpled paper, which she felt sure was the one on which Amos had been engaged.

8

It was part of an old letter, undated, but bearing every sign, in its yellowish paper, faded ink, old-fashioned handwriting, and voluminous style, of having been written long before the introduction of the penny post. The page containing the signature was missing, but the commencement, "My dear Oswin," showed that it was written to one of her ancestors—Oswin being a family name—and internal evidence proved that it was from one intimate friend to another.

The writer began by regretting that his own health was so bad, not having been improved by a long voyage he had recently taken to improve it, that he was unable to come to see his friend Oswin, who, he was sorry to hear, was also far from well. He wrote in the strain of a man who thinks the end of his own life approaching.

"And now," so the letter went on, "before the end of my own days shall come, I have somewhat on my mind which I would fain impart to you. Of late, being unable to follow my accustomed pursuits, and compelled to endure a sedentary life which suits me but ill, I have been studying the history of our own land, and more especially such part of it as concerns the reign of our late martyred King Charles, of blessed memory. In the course of my researches (if I may bestow on my poor studies so honorable a name) I have read much of the valiant defence of your own fair Castle of Carstow, that now lies ruined, and have noted a thing that may have escaped your eyes. You know, doubtless, being well versed in the history of this notable and loyal fortress, that shortly before the siege by the rebels, under Essex, the Queen Henrietta Maria did send to her own country of France a trusty messenger, charged straightly to entreat the king for help for her and her lord, and also bearing certain rich jewels of hers for sale in the Netherlands, that the proceeds thereof might be used for payment of troops. And it is known that this messenger did return in safety to England, and that he did reach Carstow, and was there detained by the siege on his way to join the king. But what became further of that noble, the Lord Hugh of Thirsk, never was known, nor was ever aught heard of the treasure he brought back or of the treasure he carried away with him. Yet was he as valiant, and trusty, and honorable a knight and gentleman as ever drew sword, nor was capable of any treachery nor unfair dealing whatsoever. But no mention of moneys reaching the king about this time was ever made, but that he was hard pressed and had to borrow and beg from his faithful courtiers is certain. Now, we know that there has always been among men, during all time, a great and most marvellous avidity for lost treasure, which appeals to the imagination most strangely, and that little of such treasure has ever been recovered. Yet, since we know that here is plain evidence of a knight, bearing treasure, reaching your Castle of Carstow; and since we have no evidence whatsoever of his being seen thereafter, or the riches he carried, is it not just to suppose that such treasure may never have left the precincts of the castle, which was then so close besieged, but that it may have been concealed from the besiegers, and thereafter either forgotten, or, the concealer being killed, its existence not known? You, with your grave discernment, not carried away by impulse, may judge my plan fantastic and unworthy your thought. But I pray you consider the suggestion I have to set before you. It is founded on a study of the castle as I made it minutely some years ago, and may lead, I think, to a discovery of importance. You will remember that, on passing under the great gateway, with its square tower to the south, you have before you a wide open space, now grass-grown, which——"

Here the bottom of the second sheet was reached, and here Marion, who was devouring the MS. with its crooked and sprawling handwriting, in the same state of feverish excitement as the librarian had suffered, was forced to a standstill.

"And the rest is in his pocket," she said to herself, with fiery impatience. "The most interesting part, too, the plan he had conceived for the finding of this treasure! I must go and find Amos Goodhare; I must force him to give it to me."

But she was spared that trouble. Springing to her feet, for she had sat down upon a pile of lumber to consider the dazzling prospect which the letter opened to her girlish imagination, she found herself face to face with the librarian himself.

The sun had gone down low in the sky while she was occupied in making out slowly, letter by letter, the old-fashioned spelling and scrawling handwriting. Now there came, through the corner of the window, the last red rays of the sunset. They fell on the face of the librarian, gave a lurid light to his grey eyes, and a diabolical cast to his complexion; so that Lady Marion, seeing him thus unexpectedly, belied her assumption of strength of mind by uttering a shrill cry. Perhaps it was the heat into which the letter had thrown her imagination; perhaps it was only the effect of the shadows thrown by the ivy outside; but it seemed to the girl that his features were distorted by passion so violent as to render him for the time scarcely human; she actually cowered as she stood, afraid that he would strike her, or that his very look would work upon her some mischief. She went through a moment of horror which she never mentioned, yet never forgot, in which the tall, spare man, with his flashing eyes and threatening attitude, the brown rafters overhead, the great piles of lumber on either side, and the thick, choking dust over all, were stamped upon her mind in a weird and vivid picture.

The next moment, as if in a dissolving view, the picture had faded away, and Amos Goodhare, the grave and courteous librarian, stood before her with his head bent and his usual stoop, in a most respectful attitude.

"I have found some papers here to-day, Lady Marion, which I believe will interest you greatly," said he in his bland, measured voice.

But Lady Marion had received a shock from which she could not in a moment recover.

"I—I—thank you. You can show me presently," she said, with dry mouth and unsteady voice.

"Can you not stay one moment, just to see one part of a letter which—ah, you have it in your hand. Have you read it? I am afraid the handwriting is not very easy to make out. Will you let me——"

"Thank you, I—I made it out," said the girl, not yet mistress of herself.

"Dear me! I am afraid I frightened you just now when I came in. I was so astonished myself to find any one in this forsaken corner, that in the dusk my imagination ran away with me, and I thought—well, I don't know exactly what I thought—but I certainly had no idea it was your ladyship who sprung up suddenly like a fairy in the darkness."

"Didn't you?" said Lady Marion, who was recovering her self-command, and had decided to come to an understanding with him at once. "I never knew that there was anything in this little recess until to-day, when I saw you come out of it to join my sister. I have read this letter—or rather the first two pages of it—and now I want you to give me the third, if you please."

There was now no mistaking the malevolence in Goodhare's eyes as he answered:

"Unfortunately I haven't got it," he said in the humblest and most deprecatory of tones. "Like a serial story, it breaks off just when one is mad for it to go on. But we must hunt and search and ransack until we find it."

"And supposing, Mr. Goodhare," suggested Lady Marion, whose temper was rising, "that you ransack first in your own pocket."

For a moment he was taken aback. The next, he smilingly turned out the contents of his coat pockets. Whether he had already stowed away the missing leaf in a safe place, or whether by some skilful sleight of hand he concealed it about his own person before her eyes, it is certain that he pulled out the lining of the very pocket into which he had so hastily thrust it, but the paper had disappeared.

"I don't know what can have made you think I had the rest of your letter, your ladyship," he said with dignity and a shade of contempt. "Any documents found in this house are the property of your family, and I hope you would scarcely accuse me of taking what is not mine. A lady's caprices must be gratified, and so I have done my best to gratify yours. At the same time I believe you will agree on reflection, that I should not be too exacting if I expected an apology."

"I do apologise, Mr. Goodhare," said Lady Marion drily. "You are so much cleverer than I thought, that I can't think of taking up any more of your time in making notes for my poor work."

And she gave him a little stiff bow as she went out.

The librarian made no answer, but a murmur of most deeply respectful apology and regret; when she had gone, however, his face puckered up with a look of malice, followed by one of anxiety.

"He would hardly dare—hardly dare, to dismiss me, I should think; and, even if he does, perhaps it may not matter now."

Again the grave, reserved face lighted up with an almost indescribable expression, in which fierce passions of hunger and yearning seemed to burst the bonds of long-continued repression and to shine forth out of a demon's eyes.

Lady Marion in the meantime had carried her grievance against the librarian straight to her mother, who, although not passionately attached to her daughters, was kind and indulgent to them. After hearing the story, she agreed to use her influence to procure the dismissal of Amos Goodhare, the more readily as she herself shared the popular prejudice against him.

"I don't promise that your father will listen to me, my dear," she said. "I dare say you are old enough to guess that Goodhare is a connection of the family, though, of course, we don't talk about it. He has to be provided for somehow, and I think your father looks upon him as rather a dangerous man—one whom he likes to keep under his own eye. Perhaps I am wrong, but that has always been my impression. And I don't suppose your father will think there is much in the story of the lost treasure."

Lady St. Austell was right. The earl pronounced the story to be "all nonsense," and said that at the beginning of the last century, to which period he assigned the letter when the first part was shown to him, people went mad on the subject of buried money, and would even fit out ships to go in search of hoards said to have been left by pirates on distant islands. However, he listened attentively to Marion's account of how she saw the librarian secrete part of the letter in his own pocket. Although he said nothing on the subject to Goodhare, perhaps he thought that his MSS. were not in safe keeping. Shortly afterwards he established a public library in the little town of Carstow, dowered it with a handsome supply of books and appointed Amos Goodhare custodian, with a small furnished house rent free and a more than ample salary.

Goodhare received news of the change in his position with his usual dignified modesty, and declared that he was entirely at the earl's service always, and was happy provided he was allowed to remain near the old town and castle of which he had grown so fond.

On learning a new regulation which Lord St. Austell, at the instance of the countess, about this time established at the old castle, Amos Goodhare, however, showed himself less submissive. The earl, who preserved all the ruins on his estates with scrupulous care, left each in charge of a keeper, who kept the key and admitted visitors on payment of a small fee. In the case of Carstow, the keeper lived in a tower of the castle itself, close to the gate. She was a respectable widow, with a family of children, and the new rule was that no person whatever should be allowed to go over any part of the ruins unaccompanied either by herself or by one of her children. The only exceptions to this regulation were the Pennant family, for whom Marion procured this privilege; and any deviation from the rule, except in their case, was to be punished by dismissal from the charge of the gate. When Amos Goodhare heard of this, he ventured, in his usual respectful manner, to suggest that this piece of favoritism would offend all the other families in the neighborhood; but the earl, who, having promised to satisfy this whim of his wife's, was not the man to go back from his word, simply said that it was known that, having no sons of his own, he took an especial interest in the Pennants; and that the regulation would be enforced in such a manner as not to interfere with the enjoyment of anybody. The rule had become necessary in consequence of the dangerous state of part of the ruins; and this reason should be published. The librarian could say no more.

But when the days grew shorter, and the black shadows of the night began to lengthen out under the grey walls early in the evening, Amos Goodhare, now installed in his little house adjoining the new library of Carstow, would spend his every spare hour in rambles round the old fortress, now this, now the other side of the winding river. Walking slowly, with eyes always cast down, and feet that appeared reluctant to rise, even for a moment, from the precious earth, he seemed to worship each blade of grass, each broken stone. It was a beautiful devotion, people said, that made a man so well known for learning and accomplishments linger so lovingly about the grey ruin, never even caring to go within the walls, but always hovering about it, scarcely letting himself go beyond the limited area within which he could keep its rugged and broken towers in view. Why, there could scarcely be a foot of ground within a mile of the castle that he didn't know, they said.

And they were right. Under the beams of the rising sun, when the laborer was going to his work in the fields; at midday, in sun, or wind, or rain; at evening time, when his work was done, and he was free to wander restlessly until far into the night, the tall, gaunt, stooping figure, with its keen, hungry eyes, stalked, like a starving ghoul, about the precincts of the castle. It passed its long, lean fingers searchingly over the very stones and among the clinging ivy that hung in ragged bunches round the bases of the towers. It crept along over the ground with shuffling, searching feet. It returned, night after night, savage and disappointed, like a starving rat to its hole.

So the winter passed.

At last, one evening in April, when every rood had been well trodden by his restless feet, Amos Goodhare gave in.

"It can't be done alone," he said to himself, bitterly. "I must have help—help."

And as he went home he made up his mind whose it should be.

CHAPTER III.

CAPTAIN PENNANT'S family was by far the most popular in the neighborhood, and this in spite of the fact that they were far too poor to give entertainments on a large scale, or to contribute largely to charities, or to do any of those things upon which popularity is generally supposed to depend.

Captain Pennant himself, though not commonly considered to be overweighted with intellect, was a gentle and chivalrous gentleman, whose strong and kindly impulses were sometimes a little disconcerting to his wife. Thus he had, on one occasion, eighteen years before, brought home from Penzance, and placed in his wife's lap, a baby girl, the orphan daughter of a fisherman who had been drowned while forming one of the crew of a life boat.

Mrs. Pennant, a stout, handsome little woman of the world, with twice her husband's common sense, and none of his straightforward simplicity of character, had at last uttered a mild protest. She was in the habit of bearing with all his caprices so beautifully, respecting his prejudices and behaving with such perfect wifely submission, that he had not the least suspicion that the grey mare was the better horse. But she was a strict Conservative, and this sudden addition to her family from the ranks of the proletariat was the last straw which broke her patience.

"I am afraid, Graham," she said, "that this dear little baby will be rather in the way in the servants' hall."

"The servants' hall!" echoed Captain Pennant, indignantly, "Alicia, I'm astonished at your suggesting such a thing. I mean the darling to be brought up as our own child."

"As our child! A fisherman's daughter!"

"We are all of the same value in the sight of heaven, Alicia," answered her husband, whose Conservatism was never allowed to interfere with his whims.

"And insects are all of the same value in our eyes. Yet we tolerate a fly where we should think a caterpillar out of place."

"Well, I don't want to know anything about flies and caterpillars, but I have adopted her as my daughter, and she is to be treated accordingly," said Captain Pennant, with increased obstinacy because of his wife's unexpected restiveness. "I believe that God has sent her to us as a precious gift and blessing, because among our own dear children we have not had a girl."

He had his own way, to all appearances, as he always had. Deborah Audaer was brought up with his sons, and treated as a young lady. But equally, of course, Mrs. Pennant had her own way more surely; for, without any overt act of unkindness, she made the girl feel, and the boys feel, that between them were no ties of blood.

Then, as they all grew up, the intriguing old lady had her punishment. For, one and all, the boys fell in love with Deborah, and when she had reached the age of nineteen they were all suitors for her hand.

Of course, the girl was true to her sex, and gave her heart where it was least wanted. Hervey, the youngest boy, a slow, broad-shouldered giant with a ruddy face and ripe-corn colored hair, who had a didactic manner and a great reputation for wisdom, was only her own age, and therefore too young for her, she said. He was a great theorist, an authority upon "style" in rowing and "seat" in riding, although he could neither pull a boat along nor stick on a horse.

A dash of the kindly prig there was about Hervey, perhaps, and a little too strong a sense that other people didn't count for much when he was about. But he was fond of Deborah, and he thought that he and she would make quite the grandest couple in the world, if only that unappreciative beast, Rees, were out of the way.

Godwin, the second son, was twenty-one; a matter-of-fact young man, of strictly moderate abilities, plenty of common sense, who never did anything that he did not do well, but in a plodding, methodical manner, without show or fuss. He had never given any trouble to anybody, and was in consequence thought very little of by anybody, particularly by his two brothers, who always exceeded their allowances while he managed to save out of his, the most meagre of the three, and who lived idly at home making up their minds "what they should be," while he had been for two years going backwards and forwards to a bank at Monmouth, where he had got himself a situation. He adored Deborah in a prosaic manner, keeping her in sweets, of which she was childishly fond, doing her shopping for her with twice as much taste and tact as she would have shown herself, and eking out the few pounds she could spare for this purpose with money of his own, so that she was filled with admiration and astonishment at his "bargains."

Deborah liked both Hervey and Godwin, but it was on Rees that she poured out all the devotion of a passionate and generous nature. Rees, the handsome, the daring, the brilliant, the favorite of the whole county, adored and indulged by his mother, petted and spoiled by Lord St. Austell, who put his horses, his dog-cart, his yacht, his guns at the service of the lad, whom he treated with smiling, good-humored fondness, as if Rees had been his own son. As a matter of course, the young fellow's character suffered from all this spoiling, as Captain Pennant, far-sighted in this matter only, had early foreboded.

"Rees is one of those unlucky lads who are born to be ruined," he had predicted, giving thereby a great shock to his wife, who was as weak as water where her eldest born was concerned, and who flattered herself, poor lady, that her prayers would counteract the effects of reckless indulgence.

At three-and-twenty Rees was the handsomest young fellow in the county. Of the middle height only and slightly built, with delicate features, curly black hair, and black eyes full of fun and fire, his appearance was irresistibly attractive to man, woman, child, and animal. His dog loved Rees with a devotion uncommon even in a dog. Careful mothers were afraid of him, for there was not a pretty girl in the countryside who would not snub the richest bachelor in the principality for the sake of the supper dance with Rees Pennant.

Nothing was difficult to him. He rode and drove well by instinct, could manage a yacht like any old salt, and always made the biggest bag at a shooting party. He had a voice pleasing without cultivation, and a laugh as musical as a bird's song. A nature so gifted, generous and genial withal, needed an armor of ideal strength of character and of intellect. Unfortunately, Rees Pennant possessed neither. The very curves of his handsome mouth betrayed weakness, which, if now excusable and even lovable, might later in life bear a pitiful significance. He was a leader and ruler now among his companions, attended by satellites of his own sex, worshipped by a troop of shy girls; but he was not of the stuff of which rulers are made, for all that.

It was on Rees Pennant that Amos Goodhare, in search of a tool and catspaw, had cast his eyes. The librarian was, perhaps, the only man in Carstow who disliked Rees; who not only saw through the lad's bright, affectionate manner to the growing selfishness and egotism beneath, but found no charm in his grace and brightness. He was, besides, intensely jealous of the earl's fondness for the young fellow, and of Deborah's passionate attachment.

For Amos had himself cast on the handsome girl eyes full of covetous longing, so that Deborah, without knowing why, blushed under his gaze and felt afraid of him.

Having decided on his plan of action, the librarian lost no time. He put himself in Rees Pennant's way one sunny April afternoon, when the latter was returning home, flushed and light-hearted, after a game of tennis on one of the Llancader lawns. The meeting took place near the top of the hilly street of which Carstow may almost be said to consist. Amos was leaning against the trunk of a tree, his soft, wide hat thrown back, his stick in his hand, as if overcome by the heat and consequent lassitude.

"Good afternoon, Mr. Pennant," he said, with that tone of flattering, dignified respect which he knew well how to assume.

"Afternoon, Goodhare," said the lad, saluting him with the airy grace peculiar to him. "Why, you look done up. Don't you like these warm spring days? They intoxicate me."

"Yes, yes," answered the elder man, putting into his grave tone an amount of respectful admiration which inclined the young fellow to stay and chat for a few minutes with the "old bookworm." "The spring suits you, and the sunshine, and girls' fair faces, and all bright things. But I'm only an old hulk, and men think me fit for nothing but to stick labels on the backs of books for fools to read and not to profit by."

"Come, that's rather hard on us Carstowites, isn't it? Some of us read seriously, you know, and how do you know we don't profit by what we read?"

"Well, Mr. Pennant, I don't want to flatter you, but you must know in your own mind that you are not like the clods around you. You have a quick brain and vivid feelings. But even you—pray excuse the liberty I am taking—show signs of the rusting effect of these narrow-hearted provincial towns. Fancy a fine young fellow like you remaining content with such a horizon! You, who might aspire to be anything you pleased—a king among men—wasting your energies on lawn tennis! Why, to me, old as I am and callous as I ought to have grown, the idea seems shocking—positively shocking!"

The young man's face had clouded slightly during this speech from the librarian, who worked himself up to a pitch of high excitement for the last words.

"How do you know that I am content?" asked Rees, quietly.

"Oh, pray forgive my taking such liberty! I got excited, carried away," murmured Amos, showing great irritation with his own indiscreet boldness.

"I'm not offended. I repeat: how do you know I'm contented?" asked Rees, swinging his tennis racquet.

"How do I know?" echoed Amos, diffidently, but with some surprise. "Why, because with natures like yours, full of energy, and fire, and daring, to will is to do. And that you have never done anything—anything great, I mean—is proof enough to me that you have never willed to do anything; that, in fact, the air of Carstow is responsible for the waste of a fine nature. Now you said you would not be offended, Mr. Pennant, and I hold you to your word."

He made a feint of moving away, but Rees detained him by a gracefully imperious gesture. The lad's complexion was flushed now with something more than the sun's heat; his candid face showed a very becoming boyish shame and modesty.

"You do me a lot more than justice, Goodhare," said he half laughing. "You make me ashamed of my own idleness, not for the first time, I do assure you, though. You see I've been spoilt; I know that; but it's so jolly that one hasn't the strength of mind to wish people wouldn't encourage one in one's evil courses."

"What evil courses? I've never heard a word about you in that way," said the librarian, whose eyes had glowed with an ugly light at this suggestion.

"Oh, nothing worse than my besetting sin, idling, which they say is the parent of all others," said Rees, looking up with his handsome, frank young face, on which was no trace of any passion worse than boyish vanity.

Goodhare's face fell, though its change of expression was not noticeable enough for his ingenuous companion to remark it.

"You see, dear old Lord St. Austell is ever so much too good to me," continued Rees with an affectionate inflection; "and while there are always his horses for me to ride and his coverts for me to shoot over, the temptation for me to do nothing else is too great."

"And why should you do anything else, at least in your leisure?" asked Goodhare, with apparent surprise. "Doesn't every gentleman who goes in for a public career in any profession amuse himself so—among other ways, of course?"

Rees laughed rather bitterly.

"Gentlemen who go in for a public career have private means, Mr. Goodhare," said he. "Everybody knows I have nothing——"

"But you are the eldest son?"

"And heir to my father's liabilities; nothing else, I assure you."

"But when you become Lady Marion's husband——"

The lad started in astonishment. The idea had never occurred to him.

"Lady Marion's husband!" he repeated, bewildered.

"Why, Mr. Pennant, you are very modest. Or don't you wish it to be talked about so soon? If so, I really beg your pardon. But you must know that it has already become common talk——"

"It's the first I've heard of it, though," said Rees, dryly. "Lord St. Austell would never let me enter Llancader Castle again if I were to hint at such a thing."

"And Lady Marion herself?" suggested the librarian, with malice.

Rees laughed rather self-consciously.

"Poor girls! They must have some creature to talk to, especially now, for this fright about scarlet fever has caused his lordship to give orders for them to remain shut up here all through the London season."

"And do you believe that, being as fond of you as his lordship is, that his daughter would not be able to talk him round?"

"I am sure she would not. I know the earl."

"So do I; and I say he would."

Rees shrugged his shoulders. He was rather impressed by the tone of quiet conviction of the elder man. After a short pause he said, hesitatingly:

"He might, perhaps, if I had money. But as it is——"

"Ah, that want of money—that fatal, miserable want of money. That's the pinch; yes, that's always the pinch," burst out Amos, with surprising energy. "How many a promising, brilliant young man—and yet not so brilliant as—well, as some I know, either—how many have been wrecked on that shoal! What might I not have done myself in the world, with the moderate abilities I have and with perseverance, if it had not been for that curse, want of money. Yes, there's the rub."

There was a pause. The younger man was lost in thought, the elder was watching him. Rees woke out of his reverie with a start, and a laugh which was, perhaps, a shade less light-hearted than usual.

"And after all," he said, shrugging his shoulders and throwing his racquet high in the air, to catch it again as easily as if he had been born a conjuror, "I don't know, when one comes to think of it, whether I would care about Lady Marion as a wife. She's a good girl, but not the most graceful creature in the world. Why, I know a girl, one who doesn't dislike me very furiously either, who has more beauty in the bend of her little finger than all the Ladies Cenarth have in their whole bodies."

Amos cast at him out of the corners of his eyes a brief glance instinct with venom.

"I don't suppose there are many girls about, high or low, who do dislike you very furiously, Mr. Pennant," he said, in a tone of sly malice not altogether as pleasing as the words; "but I do earnestly hope, if I may presume to say so, that you will not destroy chances which I, an old experienced man, perceive to be great, for the sake of a pretty face in a rank of life beneath you."

"You may be quite sure that the girl I should choose for a wife would be beneath nobody, Goodhare," said Rees, with haughtiness in which there was no offence. "But anyhow," he added, with another laugh, "there's time enough to think about that. I don't mean to bestow upon any lady my name and my tennis racquet—all I possess—for the next ten years."

"Of course not. You mean to enjoy yourself."

Rees did not quite understand the significance of the elder man's tone, but it rather grated on him.

"Yes, I mean to enjoy myself in my own way," he said, as he sprang up from the gate on which he had been sitting, and prepared to continue his walk. "Well, good night, Goodhare; I must be getting home."

"Good night, Mr. Pennant. I wish you'd come round to the library some evening and see an edition of Carlyle which I've just had rebound after my own taste. I'm rather proud of it. It won't be very entertaining for you, but it will bring a ray of sunshine into my grey life, and show me that you are not offended by my frankness."

He had touched on the right chord again. The young fellow held out his hand and grasped that of the librarian warmly.

"Of course I'll come," he said good humoredly. "Only you mustn't butter me up so; it'll turn my head."

He ran down the hill like the boy he still was, and turned his handsome young face for a farewell nod to Goodhare as he reached the bottom.

Amos returned the salutation, but Rees was too far off to hear his suppressed chuckle of hideous exultation.

"He takes the bait already," he said to himself, grinding out the words between his teeth. "What a pitiful fool he is, and how splendidly he'll suit my purpose."

CHAPTER IV.

IT was about three months after the first friendly interview between Rees Pennant and Amos Goodhare that, one hot July afternoon, Deborah Audaer was sitting on the terrace behind Captain Pennant's house, with a book in her hand, and her eyes fixed, not upon its pages, but upon the straggling, untrimmed fruit trees which filled the bottom of the garden.

Everything about the place—the glimpse of shabby furniture inside the open French window behind her, the greenish flags and broken balustrade of the terrace, and wild and uncultivated condition of the long garden—told of limited means and a pitiful struggle to make both ends meet. Deborah herself was dressed in the most extraordinarily ill-fitting frock that ever clothed a beautiful girl. It was made of a pretty bluish-grey cotton, and set off between the throat and the left shoulder by a bunch of double poppies. But it was too tight in front, too loose in the back, garnished everywhere by unexpected puckers, and giving the idea that it was making its wearer very uncomfortable. Deborah, who was tall and of a handsome, well-developed figure, looked in this garment as if she was masquerading in the dress of a narrow-chested girl with a hump-back. However, her fresh beauty was too decided to be spoilt by such an accident; she had a rich brunette complexion, blue eyes, good teeth, a nose a little bit inclined to be aquiline, and dark-brown hair with strands of a bright copper color.

She had been sitting idly, with rather a melancholy expression of face, for some time, when Godwin, who had been watching the back of her head from the open window, stepped out on to the terrace and seated himself on the balustrade in front of her.

It was not surprising that a young girl should find him less attractive than Rees, for Godwin was short, sallow, insignificant of feature, and rather brusque in manner.

"What are you thinking about, Deborah?" he asked with a shrewd look.

"Nothing," of course, she answered promptly.

"That is a—well, a perversion of the truth. You were thinking of Rees."

"I suppose I can think of anything I like."

"Yes, provided—firstly, that you tell the truth about it; and, secondly, that you don't lose your temper over it. Shall I give another guess, and tell you *what* you thought about Rees?"

"You can if you like," said she with an affectation of indifference.

But she turned away to hide the fact that tears were rising to her eyes.

"Well, we won't talk any more about him," said he hastily, distressed and irritated that she should cry over what he considered an unworthy object.

22

"Yes, we will," cried Deborah, turning suddenly and almost fiercely. "I can't bear it all by myself any longer; and you, Godwin, who understand things, you can perhaps tell me what is the matter."

"With Rees?"

"Yes. He's changed lately, changed altogether; it's been coming on gradually, but it's been most plain the last month or six weeks. Haven't you noticed it?"

"I've noticed that he's become ill-tempered and discontented, and doesn't seem to think any of us good enough for him."

"Well, he used not to be like that, you know, he used not. He was always bright and cheerful and happy. But ever since he's taken this studious fit, which we thought at first was such a good thing, he's quite changed. He seems to avoid me, and everybody; and I've heard him say such ungrateful things of Lord St. Austell, who's been so good to him. And yet now, when he isn't shut up reading in his own room or up at the library in the town, he's always up at Llancader."

"Don't you know why?" asked Godwin, drily.

The girl grew a little paler and her breath came faster, as if she had an idea that she was to hear something unpleasant. But she did not answer.

"Of course you'll hate me for telling you," said Godwin rather bitterly. "And it's no use to tell you it's for your own good. Anyhow, it's this: Rees is making up to Lady Marion. I've told him he's only making a fool of himself, and I've got snubbed for my pains. There."

But Deborah had drawn herself up with haughty astonishment.

"And why shouldn't he 'make up' to Lady Marion? He's a great deal too good for any of those silly, conceited girls."

Godwin looked at her attentively.

"Girls *are* ridiculous creatures," he said at last, contemptuously. "They'll like a man without reason, and they'll go on liking him against reason. However, we won't talk about Rees any more, except that I'll just say this: 'Use all your influence with him to try to get him to turn his hand to something; for I'm inclined to think this illness of my poor father's is more serious than we like to believe, and if anything happens to him Rees and Hervey will have to put their shoulders to the wheel, for father's pension ends with his life, and his affairs are in a hopeless state of muddle. Now, don't cry; it had to be said, and if I haven't said it in the best way you must forgive me."

But Deborah's tears were flowing fast. There was only one person in the world whom she loved as well as Rees, and that was Captain Pennant. The idea of his death, which had forced itself upon her again and again lately, she could never bear calmly.

"Now, I thought you had more sense than to give way like that," said Godwin, trying to be very stern. "I look to you to help me to comfort my mother, who hasn't the least notion of what you and I—know."

Deborah shook her head.

"She won't let me comfort her. She has never—never looked upon me as anything but an intruder, and when our poor father dies I shall have to go. It is only right, too, of course. It's only lately I've begun to see and know what a burden I must have been upon them all these years——"

"Nonsense, Deb. You may be sure my father—and all of us—never considered you that."

"Of course he didn't, he is too good," said the girl, with a caressing tone. "But it's true, all the same. And you needn't look like that at me. I shall be glad to earn my own living, and I don't care how. See, I've begun to make my own dresses; I made this one."

With the tears still rolling down her cheeks, she sat upright with some pride.

"The back of the bodice looks a little like the waves of the sea in a pantomime," said Godwin, who was a critic on the subject of woman's dress. "However, no doubt the intention was better than the sewing." Then he came to a sudden stop, and presently said, "There's something else to be thought of when you talk about going away. You know we all want to marry you."

"Rees doesn't," burst from her lips.

The next moment she hung her head, crimson and confused.

But Godwin took this outburst beautifully.

"He couldn't just now, however much he wanted to," said he, soothingly. "But he will by-and-bye, if he isn't even a more thundering idiot than I think him," he added with a burst of irritation. "And if he shouldn't——"

She interrupted him hastily, with a look almost of fear in her eyes, as she put her hand affectionately on his arm.

"Look here, Godwin," she began hurriedly. "I know what you're going to say; but you mustn't say it. It's of no use pretending things to you, for you notice everything. Well, and you know I love Rees, and I'm not ashamed of it—no, not a bit," she added, raising her blushing face fearlessly to his. "He has faults, I know, but there is enough good in him to love, and I do love him. And if he marries any other girl I shall never marry at all; but if he ever marries me, even if he were to be always cross and cold to me, as he has been lately, and if he were to lose all his handsomeness and brightness, and be miserable, and old, and dull, I should be happier as his wife than as the wife of the best man that ever lived."

"Oh, of course; I don't doubt it. A good character in a man is a scarecrow which would frighten any woman away."

"You don't believe me?"

"Yes, I do, unfortunately. I always had a secret belief that girls were idiots. Now it's an open belief. That's all."

Deborah rose, and leaned over the balustrade, against which Godwin was kicking his heels and knocking off pieces of the mouldering stone.

"I can't help it, Godwin," she said, with a sigh.

"And I can't help being just as fond of you as if you were a woman of sense," said he, with another sigh. "And the worst of it is, that loving you has reduced me to your own level. For I know that there isn't any hope for me, and that all the same I shall go on hoping, so that, without any fault on your side or my side, you will be the bane of my life."

"Oh, Godwin, how can you say such dreadful things?" said the girl, with a scared face.

"You will forget them, and everything else—as soon as Rees comes in," said Godwin, bitterly.

Before she could utter another protest, he had gone back into the house, leaving Deborah unhappy and self-reproachful. And yet those last words of his were true, as she knew. Lord St. Austell, who had been in town for the season, was expected to arrive at Llancader that day for a short stay, before joining his yacht for a long cruise. Rees had been so feverishly anxious to meet him that Deborah had become deeply interested as to the object of the interview. That Rees was not actuated merely by gratitude and affection she knew, as he had been lately in the habit of casting on the earl all the blame of his own idleness.

The fact was that Amos Goodhare, having devoted himself to the study of Rees Pennant's character, and especially of its weaknesses, had managed by degrees to get such a hold upon him, and to use it in such a diabolical manner, that the lad's good impulses were being gradually choked and the evil encouraged, while even the loving women of his own household were unable to trace the true source of the change, the effects of which were plain to one at least of them.

Swallowing the bait which the cunning Goodhare held out to his vanity, he persistently avoided Deborah, for whom he had a natural inclination, and hung about Marion, whose unabashed adoration at heart rather disgusted than attracted him. Why should he not become the earl's son-in-law, as the librarian, by insinuation rather than by direct speech, so constantly suggested? Lord St. Austell had no sons, and had never shown for any man, young or old, so great a partiality as he constantly did for him. He was handsome, brilliant, and more like the ideal conception of what a nobleman's son ought to be than any eldest son in the whole aristocracy. Rees knew this, and felt more than a modest confidence in the fact. He even began to think that in the earl's constant indulgence, which had indeed greatly increased the lad's aversion from the thought of serious work, he saw a long-fixed determination to provide for his future in some brilliant manner.

So that, by the time of the earl's return to Llancader, Rees had quite prepared himself for an encouraging answer to his proposals. He went to meet him at the station, and everything seemed to favor his wishes. Lord St. Austell was more than kind, he was most affectionate in his greeting, in his inquiries after all the family, not forgetting Deborah. Then, saying that he would like a walk, he dismissed the dog-cart that had been sent to meet him, and, thrusting his arm through that of Rees, started with him towards Llancader.

Nothing could be more propitious, so thought Rees, who felt too hopeful to spoil his effect by rushing at the subject. It was not until they were in sight of the first lodge that Rees, emboldened to make a very spirited appeal, formally asked the earl's consent to his marriage with Lady Marion.

Lord St. Austell listened in complete, attentive silence. Rees thought it was all right, when, at the end of his carefully prepared and beautifully delivered speech, the earl burst into a fit of laughter.

"Oh, you boys and girls!" he said, indulgently, but with great amusement, "when will you learn a little sense?"

And again he began to laugh.

When Rees had recovered from his first impulse of rage and mortification, he asked, in his haughtiest manner—

"Am I to understand from this strange reception that you refuse my proposals?"

"No, no, dear boy, we won't put it like that," said the earl, seeing that he had hurt the young fellow's feelings, and laying on his shoulder a kindly hand, which Rees instantly shook off, as if by an accidental stumble. "We'll forget all about it, we'll decide that you never for a moment dreamt of such folly as asking for one of my poor dowerless, unattractive girls. Why, lad, what would you live on?"

"I may be rich some day," said Rees quietly.

"Well, well, so you may, and then you can marry a beautiful woman, and treat her a great deal better than most of us treat our wives. And mind, my boy, I like the impulse which made you feel you would like to be something nearer to me; for that, I am sure, was what first put this mad notion into your head. And I have a proposal to make to you, which I hope may lead to something more satisfactory than this unlucky one of yours. I have an opening for a steward on my Midland property, and you, with your love of the open air, and of riding and driving, would find it an easy and pleasant berth. I need not tell you that I should treat you in a very different spirit from that which I should show to anybody else. And I should overlook any shortcomings which might arise from want of experience——"

"You may save yourself the trouble of making excuses for me, my lord," interrupted Rees, whose handsome face was white with passion. "You will not have me for a son-in-law; well, at any rate, you shall not have me for a servant, and I wish your ugly daughters better husbands."

Lord St. Austell looked up in pain and amazement. But Rees had left him, and was speeding back towards Carstow. The earl's face grew very grave as he asked himself what miracle could have wrought such a hideous change in the frank, generous-spirited lad.

In the meantime, Rees reached the little town, still in a tempest of passion. He called in at the library; Goodhare was out. He hurried home, dashed through the garden, and into the house by one of the back windows, without noticing that there seemed to be an unusual silence and stillness about the place. A servant whom he met ran out of his way, as if afraid to meet him. Deborah burst out crying at sight of him, and tried to detain him at the foot of the stairs. But she could not speak, and after waiting by her side impatiently for a few seconds, Rees gently pushed her aside, and mounted the staircase to his mother's room.

With her he was sure of sympathy, no matter what he had done; no matter, too, how much in the wrong he might be.

He burst open the door, and dashed into the room.

Mrs. Pennant was there, but she was not sitting as usual, knitting in her low armchair by the window. She had his father's desk on her knees, and was busy, with Godwin, reading over the papers it contained. Her eyes were red with crying, but her face wore a set, stern expression of responsibility and anxiety. Godwin also looked sad and anxious. Both mother and son started at his abrupt entrance, and the former, holding out her arms towards him, tried to smile as she asked him where he had been.

"To meet Lord St. Austell," answered Rees, bewildered by the strange reception he met with from every one. "And what do you think, mother, he presumed to offer me?"

"I don't know, my dear boy," said Mrs. Pennant, caressing his curly head with a trembling hand.

"He wanted me to become his steward—his land steward. What do you think of that?"

Godwin sprang up from the seat by his mother's side.

"For heaven's sake, Rees, don't tell us you were such a fool as to refuse?"

"I did refuse, of course. It is not for me, the prospective head of the Pennant family, to become the paid dependent of any man."

"Well, it's better than being a pauper, head of the family or not. And that's what mother and I have just discovered you to be."

Mrs. Pennant's tears began to flow again.

"He is right, Rees, I am afraid," said she, in a sad, low voice. "Your father never would let us know the real state of his affairs, and we have just found out enough to make us fear that we are absolutely ruined."

Rees looked from one face to the other in utter bewilderment. His mother drew his head tenderly to her breast.

"Your poor father, Rees, fell down dead in the drawing-room two hours ago."

Rees tore himself from his mother's clasp with wild eyes. For a moment he saw the reckless folly of the course he had been pursuing, and the ruin to which it had brought him. The next, his mind was again clouded. For the poison of delicate flattery had been subtle, and had penetrated his system thoroughly.

Half an hour later he was walking up the hill, with unsteady steps, towards Amos Goodhare's lodgings.

CHAPTER V.

REES PENNANT reached Amos Goodhare's lodgings just as the latter, having finished his tea, was about to start on his usual evening walk.

He saw the young man coming up the street, and waited on the threshold for him, noting, with hawk-like keenness, the signs of unusual and strong emotion in his ingenuous face.

"Come in, come in, my dear young friend," he said with soothing deference, which poured balm into poor Rees's wounded soul. "I am fortunate, indeed, to have delayed starting just long enough to see you."

And he stood aside, inviting the young man to enter with a welcoming gesture.

Rees hurried in, threw himself on the little, hard, chintz-covered sofa in the cottage sitting-room, and tried to bury his face in the one brick-like cushion. Goodhare followed him into the room, and, without worrying him by persistent inquiries into the cause of his evident distress, stood beside the couch and placed a firm hand, the very touch of which seemed to the unhappy lad instinct with friendship and support, on the young fellow's shoulder.

The room faced the east, and the light from the window was, moreover, obscured by a screen of long-legged geranium plants. When, therefore, Rees suddenly turned and looked up at the librarian, he did not notice the hungry impatience in the elder man's eyes, like the expression of a vulture hovering over the body of a dying traveller. He saw only the tall figure bending over him, felt only the pressure of a long, lean hand on his, and believed that here at last was some one who understood him, who loved him, not with the blind, unreasoning love of his mother and Deborah, but with affection and admiration which were a just tribute to his own high qualities. Here he should find true sympathy, unmixed with blame.

"Something is troubling you, my dear boy, if you will allow me to call you so," said Amos, at last, in a voice the very tones of which were consolation. "Tell me if you like, or be silent if you like. You can take your own time with—if I may presume to call myself so—an old friend like me."

"Thanks, Goodhare, thanks a thousand times," said Rees; and wringing the librarian's hand with a strong, warm pressure, he sprang up, tossed back his curly hair, and held up a frank, young face, convulsed with a dozen emotions which he in vain tried to hide, to the shrewd gaze of the elder man.

"The fact is, you must know—or perhaps you *do* know—that I've been making an arrant fool of myself. I don't know how it was that I didn't see it before, but I see it now with a clearness that's positively appalling."

29

He sat down, and leaned forward on his elbows with clasped hands and an expression of utter hopelessness. Amos waited in respectful silence, and presently Rees continued—

"First of all, my poor father's dead. He died of heart disease this afternoon, and that was the news that greeted me when I returned home this evening, after receiving the greatest blow to my feelings—to my vanity, if you like—that I've ever had to put up with."

"Poor boy!" murmured Amos compassionately.

"Secondly, we are 'broke,' absolutely without the pounds, shillings, and pence necessary to pay for bread and butter, coals and candles, let alone such extras as rent and clothing. That's pretty bad, isn't it? But worse remains behind." He was trying to recover his old bright manner, and to face his difficulties with some appearance of courage. "For I have the satisfaction of knowing that it's my own fault that I am not to-day in possession of prospects of supporting my family in a much more comfortable manner than before. That's not exactly a comfortable frame of mind, is it?"

"Why, no, I'm afraid it is not. But surely you exaggerate——"

"Not a bit of it. And you've only heard about half. The last and worst point is that I've quarrelled with my best friend, and in such a manner that even the most grovelling apology would scarcely put me right with him again."

Goodhare had listened with his head half turned away, in the attitude of deep attention, to his young friend's recital; the glow of satisfaction in his eyes as each misfortune was named thus escaped his hearer's observation. But when he heard the last, the crowning source of distress, Amos, old as he was, could only conceal the passionate, evil joy he felt by an abrupt change of position. Rising hastily, as if overcome by the sad intelligence, he went to the window and looked out into the little stony street, while visions of ill-gotten gold floated before his eyes, and sounds of the boisterous revelry, for which his corrupt soul hankered in age as it had hankered in youth, made hideous but welcome music in his ears. It was with a start he turned, as his companion's voice broke in upon his reverie.

"Well, what do you think of my position now?"

Amos had to think a moment before he spoke. For in the glowing picture he had conjured up, the poor tool had been forgotten. Then, with measured steps, he crossed the little room, and sat down by Rees.

"Tell me," he said sympathetically, "if you will so far honor me with your confidence, how this disastrous state of things came about."

Rees told him the whole story faithfully, not withholding the record of his own shame and astonishment, and the mortifying derision with which the earl had received his proposals. He had expected sympathy, he had expected a kindly palliation of his own fault. But he was not prepared for the torrent of outraged amazement with which Goodhare heard the account of Lord St. Austell's behavior.

The librarian walked to and fro on the hearth-rug, which was the longest promenade his tiny sitting-room afforded.

"To think that he, of all men, after the admiration he always expressed for you, the hints which he has frequently given about the handsome manner in which he intended to provide for you"—here Rees looked up in surprise,—"that he should treat you in this manner, as if you were his inferior! I cannot understand it! I always imagined him to be a man of right feeling and noble instincts, incapable of outraging the feelings of a man poorer than himself."

"Well," said Rees, who, now that his own cause was espoused so hotly, could afford to be magnanimous, "money makes the one great difference now, you know, as Lord St. Austell has said himself a dozen times."

Amos stopped suddenly in the centre of the hearth-rug.

"If you could only, some day, get rich, make a fortune, and come back and see him anxious for you to renew your proposal! What a revenge that would be for you!"

The young man looked at him dubiously. Even to the excitable brain of twenty-three, that seemed a fantastic and melodramatic idea.

"Yes," he answered, rather drily, "but fortunes are not picked up in the roads."

"Not often," assented Amos, watching him. "Yet still I have heard of money being picked up in strange ways."

"It isn't likely to come much in my way, though, unless indeed I eat humble pie, and beg his lordship to give me the—the place, I suppose you call it, which I refused to-day so contemptuously."

"And are you really ready to do that?" asked Amos, in a tone so full of scorn that the weak and sensitive lad writhed under it.

"As ready as I am to starve, perhaps," answered he, reddening.

"But why do either?" asked the librarian, in a low, soft tone of gentle persuasion. "Providence does sometimes favor the deserving, and though I am not superstitious, I am inclined to think that, having preserved you from a life of unworthy drudgery, such as your own family seem to have been quite willing for you to adopt, Providence has some better destiny in store for you than you fancy."

"Providence had better make haste about it then, or she may find that she has missed her chance."

"Shall we take a walk together?" asked Amos, who began to see in the lad's eyes the look of desperation he had been hoping for. "The fresh air sometimes cools the brain, and gives one fresher and brighter thoughts. It is my sovereign remedy for all the ills of my dull life. Come."

Rees let himself be led out by the librarian; but when the latter wished to direct his steps towards the ruins of Carstow Castle, he drew back and protested.

"Not to the castle. I don't want to go to any place which reminds me of that man and the humiliation he put me to to-day."

"Try to get over that feeling," insisted Amos, gently drawing him forward in the direction of the old walls. "Take my word for it, the humiliation will some day be on the other side. Besides, the old castle can hardly be called his property. Any treasure found buried in the ruins would not be his; it would belong to that vague thing, 'the Crown.'"

"Treasure!" echoed Rees, astonished. "Why, surely you don't believe that cock-and-bull story Lady Marion told me! Lord St. Austell himself said that every ruin in the three kingdoms had some such story attached to it, as surely as the ivy."

"That doesn't prove that it may not sometimes be well authenticated. As a matter of fact, in this case I believe it to be so."

"Have you told the earl?"

"When I hinted my belief it was received with derision. So I have kept it to myself till now."

"With derision, do you say? But Lady Marion thought there was something in the story. And she thought you had kept back part of the story."

"So I had. It would have been of no use to Lady Marion; so far, indeed, it has been none to me. But with your help——"

"You don't count on my help for a robbery, surely!" interrupted Rees with much haughtiness.

"No. Of what use would it be for anybody to count upon your help in a dishonorable action? I am not so stupid. But I do think that you will not refuse your assistance in discovering the treasure, if indeed it should exist, which is, as you say, by no means certain. The search will be an arduous one, and will require the exercise of qualities of no common order. But if something should come of it, think what a splendid opportunity you would have of heaping coals of fire on the head of the man who insulted you so lightly to-day. That, indeed, would be a noble revenge, and his lordship could hardly, in common gratitude, do less than accept you for a son-in-law if you put in his hands such a handsome supply of ready money."

"But if this apocryphal treasure really existed, and were discovered by us, how do you know what its amount would be? And what good would it do to Lord St. Austell if buried treasure goes, as you say, to the Crown?"

"The treasure, if it exists, consists either in the jewels—royal jewels, mind, which Henrietta Maria sent to the Netherlands to be sold—or in the proceeds of that sale, which, it was expected, would be sufficient to wipe off long arrears of debt to a whole army and to pay for the levying of fresh troops. Now only two-thirds of a buried treasure are claimed by the Crown. Wouldn't the remaining third of such a sum as that be a comfortable little windfall?"

"I dare say it would," answered Rees hastily. For he was anxious to get rid of a subject which he felt to contain a temptation to his honor. "But as you have conceived the idea of this find being possible, I don't think I ought to step in at the last moment and rob you of part of the honor of it."

"But it is not the last moment; it is, on the contrary, only the first step that we have reached—that of recognising the fact that there may be treasure there, and that, if there is, it can only be reached from the inside of the castle walls."

"From the inside?" echoed Rees in spite of himself, interested in the ever-fascinating suggestion, and impressed by the growl of passionate, hungry earnestness in the elder man's hawk eyes.

"Yes. And as only the members of your family are allowed to ramble over the ruins without a guide nobody but you can pursue the search. Do you see?"

"That is unfortunate," said Rees, with the irascible decision of the weak, who never feel that they have sufficiently emphasised the determination which they doubt their power to keep.

"For nothing would induce me to take advantage of a favor shown to me. Besides," he added, after a lame pause, which Amos did not attempt to break, "after this afternoon's work, of course Lord St. Austell will retract his special permission to my family."

"He won't think of it," said Amos quietly. "And if he did, he wouldn't condescend to do so."

"And I shall certainly not show myself less magnanimous than he," said Rees.

Again Goodhare said nothing; and again it was Rees who had to break the silence. It was rather awkward to do so, but curiosity concerning this project of the librarian's began to burn within him.

"What makes you so strong in this belief, Goodhare? It isn't like you to take an infatuation without good reason to back it."

"There were nearly always, at the period when Carstow Castle was last rebuilt, subterranean passages built through which the occupants could escape in case of a surprise."

"But, if there had been, would not the garrison have used these passages to escape by, when they were hard pressed, during the siege?"

"The surmise is that these passages, not having been used for many years, were believed to be impracticable. If they existed at all, this was probably the case, as I have searched the neighborhood thoroughly for nearly a mile in every direction round the castle, and I can find no trace of any opening."

"And don't you think what that proves is that there never was either passage or opening?"

"I do not. I believe that this unlucky Lord Hugh, knowing the heavy responsibility which lay on his shoulders, may have tried this means of escape, and been buried in the attempt with whatever he carried, whether jewels or money. How else—in what more reasonable manner can you account for his utter disappearance? For that neither he, nor the money he had been sent to fetch, ever reached the king, is certain."

"I should think any manner of accounting for his disappearance likelier than that one," said Rees. "And even if that were the true explanation, nothing would induce me to prowl about Lord St. Austell's property to find out the truth of it."

He said this haughtily, yet he waited when he had finished speaking, to hear Goodhare's further arguments.

But the elder man had apparently decided that to argue against such flinty determination would be waste of breath. He turned away from the young man with a sigh.

"Well, Mr. Pennant, it is no use for me to try to persuade you into any course which you do not think strictly honorable, I know. I will, therefore, say no more about this, but only ask you to believe that I would never have breathed a word on the matter to you, if I had not myself believed it to be a suggestion which you might follow up to your own honor and Lord St. Austell's profit."

"I don't wish to do anything to his profit," said Rees passionately. "But, of course, I know you meant well, and—and thank you, and—and good-night."

He gave Goodhare's hand a grateful squeeze, and then lingered as if expecting a little more argument or a little more persuasion from him.

But none came. Goodhare simply wished him good-night, and left him to return home by himself with slow steps and an unusually reflective manner.

When he got home he found that his practical brother, Godwin, and his harassed mother, had had time to make a more thorough examination of such of his father's papers as were within their reach, and that the result, even of this cursory search, was worse than they had feared. Nothing but debts, debts; bills unpaid, liabilities unmet. It was ruin, absolutely ruin, without a hope. Rees had to learn the truth, from their haggard eyes first, and their lips afterwards. Poor, kind-hearted old Captain Pennant had not been of so much account in the world or in his own household but that this discovery of the penniless state in which he had left his family overshadowed their grief at his death.

Rees listened to the recital at first in dumb dismay. Then came a feeling of bitterness, of injury. Lastly, the idea of the gold which might lie hidden among those old ruins within half a mile of his own wrecked home rushed into his brain, not as the chimerical vision it had appeared when Amos first mentioned it to him that evening, but as a vivid, saving truth. So fast had the welcome fancy grown unconsciously in his mind.

At ten o'clock that night, when the quiet little town lay already asleep, and the bats were flying in the moonlight about the ragged walls of Carstow Castle, Rees crept out of his home like a guilty creature, and ran along the quiet roads and lanes with a fast-beating heart, until he stopped under the old portcullis, and leaned, panting for breath, against the massive oak door, which, studded with huge nails, and held together by thick bars of rusty iron, had stood the test of centuries of hard usage, and still kept intruders out of the ruin as it had kept them out of the castle in the time of its strength and its prime.

What were the secrets it held within its keeping? Was there indeed gold, in handfuls, in sackfuls, buried behind its jealous barrier?

Rees Pennant's brain was growing heated under the spell which the glittering fancy cast upon him. With stealthy feet he soon was pacing underneath the walls, as Amos Goodhare had done the winter and the summer long, now caressing the rugged old stones, now tearing away the ivy which covered them, maddened by that idea of hidden treasure to be had for the finding, which has played havoc with the reason of stronger men.

He saw no one on his stealthy walk. But he was not unseen.

At the angle of the ancient wall, Amos Goodhare, to whom this nightly prowling was now an accustomed thing, suddenly caught sight of this new searcher in the darkness. He drew back hastily into the shadow of the trees, where his eyes seemed to blaze luridly out of the surrounding blackness as he laughed to himself silently.

"Caught, caught, my little fly," he thought, with the nod of a triumphant fiend. "There we are—a step nearer to my gold, *my* gold!"

Rees came on, and passed him, feeling the old walls with feverish hands, and unluckily not seeing Amos, nor the expression with which his friend and mentor gloated over his boyish eagerness.

So, turning his back reluctantly to the castle and its grim grey towers, Rees crept, in a fever of longing and high excitement, back to his home.

CHAPTER VI.

MRS. PENNANT was a woman of some strength of character, which had never before come out so vividly as it did on the occasion of her husband's death.

She spent very little time in weeping over his loss. She was one of those women in whom the instincts of maternal affection are much stronger than the marital; and in truth her patience had been so hardly tried by Captain Pennant's almost imbecile mismanagement of his affairs and the necessity of controlling her exasperation into the outer aspect of submissive respect, that there was a touch of relief even in her sorrow.

The few days between the death and the funeral were passed by all in an uneasy state of apprehension as to what would follow. Rees was hardly ever in the house, and could not be approached on the subject of his future actions. Hervey mooned about, comforting himself, after his usual fashion, by great thoughts of life and death, and the impracticable things he would do to get his family out of their difficulties. Godwin went quietly backwards and forwards to the bank as usual. Deborah kept out of Mrs. Pennant's way, believing, poor child, that as that lady had never liked her, and had only suffered her to remain a member of the household in consequence of the captain's express wish, she should now be ignominiously expelled on the first decent opportunity.

Deborah was Captain Pennant's truest mourner. During the days when he lay dead in the house, she spent most of her time watching by his coffin, gazing at the passionately loved face of her "father," as she had always called him, and grieving over her loss with all the intensity of her fiercely loving nature. The remaining hours of her time she spent, not in luxurious regret at leaving the old house which had so long been her home, but in looking over the clothes of the boys and mending such as wanted repairs, and in doing every little bit of active work she could think of to save Mrs. Pennant trouble. She did not love Mrs. Pennant; sometimes she had felt she almost hated her; but she appreciated the sense of duty to her husband which had made the lady tolerate her presence, and she felt bound to make what small return she could before breaking what she believed to be to the elder lady a galling tie.

So, on the day after the funeral, Deborah presented herself early in the day before Mrs. Pennant in her walking dress. The elder lady was writing at the table, and the girl stood for some moments watching her, without speaking; she was a good deal affected by the prospect of parting, now that it was so near, more especially as she noticed that Mrs. Pennant had aged suddenly, and that her handsome face showed the lines and wrinkles brought by care and anxiety more clearly than ever before. At last Mrs. Pennant looked up.

"Oh, are you going out, Deborah? Would you mind taking these letters to the post for me? I have just finished."

Deborah murmured assent, and Mrs. Pennant bent over her writing. As she closed the last envelope, she looked up again. The girl stepped forward and quietly took up the letters. Then, turning to go, she addressed Mrs. Pennant without facing her, for she was afraid of breaking down, and bringing upon herself a cold reproof.

"I am going away, mamma. I came in to say good-bye to you. I am afraid you will not believe me when I say I am sorry to leave you; you think me ungrateful, but I am not. I am afraid I have been a burden on you for a great many years; but, thanks to your goodness, I can support myself now. I shall never forget you, or the boys, or—or my dear, dear father—I mean Captain Pennant."

Mrs. Pennant was entirely taken aback. It was not until this moment that she knew how much she should miss the bright, beautiful face, or how lonely she should feel without the girl whom, in spite of herself, she had long secretly looked upon as a daughter.

"This, this is very sudden. You might have spoken to me. I had a right to expect to be consulted," she said, trying to speak coldly, but with a tremor in her voice.

"I didn't know how—I didn't like to trouble you," faltered the girl.

"Where are you going to? What do you want to do?"

"I have got a situation as help, lady-help they call it, at a little town the other side of Monmouth."

"Lady—help! A girl brought up as Captain Pennant's daughter!" cried the poor lady, in disgust and dismay.

"Well, mamma, what could I do? I should never have had the patience to teach children; and I can cook and sew a little, and I'm sure I could scrub. Nobody will ever know me as Captain Pennant's daughter any more," she said sadly. "I am simply Deborah Audaer, the fisherman's daughter."

"But you can't go back like that, it's impossible," said Mrs. Pennant pettishly. "You are a lady now, whatever you were born. And my husband adopted you as his daughter, so his daughter you will always be to me. And you must remain with me. Understand that."

She spoke sharply and querulously, but with determination. Still Deborah stood before her, looking perturbed and undecided.

"Do you hear what I say?" asked the old lady, peremptorily.

"Yes, I hear, mamma," answered Deborah, in a low-toned, broken voice. Then, after a moment's further hesitation, she moved two steps nearer, sank down on her knees, and hid her face in Mrs. Pennant's chair. "Mamma," she whispered, "I can't stay—if you speak to me like that. You must try to be fond of me, and I'll stay, and be good to you, work for you if I can, comfort you if I can. You would never let me love you before—will you try now? Captain Pennant is gone, Rees doesn't care for me now; I can't live without any love, in the place where I had so much. I would rather go away among strangers; I could bear that better."

Mrs. Pennant was touched. At last she felt her heart go out to the brave, frank girl, and she put a trembling hand upon her neck, where the soft brown hair strayed from under the sombre black bonnet.

"Stay, child," she whispered. "You shall not have to complain."

Half a word was enough for Deborah, craving, as she did, an affection to replace what she had lost. She threw her strong young arms round her with a clasp in which the poor harassed lady felt at last not only comfort, but support. And from that hour Deborah transferred, if not all, at least a great part of the affection she had felt for her adopted father to his widow, whom she cherished and served with a true daughter's devotion.

Meanwhile, the unhappiest member of the household was poor Rees, who, before his father had been dead a week, found that his own position as head of the family had been practically usurped by his younger brother Godwin. This shrewd and energetic fellow, on learning Lord St. Austell's offer to Rees and the latter's refusal of it, had instantly been seized with the idea of applying himself for the post.

The earl was rather cold at first, feeling, on account of Rees's conduct, a temporary disgust with the whole family. But Godwin insisted so humbly, representing truly enough that he had had, young as he was, much more business experience than his elder brother, that at last he gained his point to the extent of being appointed assistant steward on trial.

When Rees learnt this, although he tried to congratulate his brother, and to wish him God-speed on his journey northwards, he fell into a passion of remorse and anger, and, rushing out of the house towards the spot which he now began to haunt as regularly as Goodhare himself, he flung himself down under the trees in a large field which stretched under the western wall of the castle, and burying his face in his hands, gave himself up to a paroxysm of despair.

What had he done, he the spoiled favorite of the county, who had begun to look upon all men's indulgence as his right, that he should suddenly find himself thrown down from his long-established position, an exile from Llancader, cut by all its inmates, neglected by Goodhare, and even avoided by his faithful slave, Deborah? For the girl's spirit had at last rebelled against his curt assumption of indifference towards her; while, as for Amos, he had had reasons for his own for giving the young man a wide berth for a few days. Those few days, however, were now over; and that very afternoon Amos, having seized the opportunity of his dinner-hour for a prowl round the goal of his dreams, saw the young fellow as he lay stretched on the grass, and instantly decided that the time was ripe for another step. He came down to the lower ground, therefore, and called Rees gently by his name before the young fellow had heard his footsteps.

The lad sprung up with a flushed, wild face and reckless manner.

"Goodhare," cried he, hoarsely, "I'll begin hunting to-night, this very night."

The elder man smiled gravely, and stroked his beard in a meditative manner.

"You have decided, then, to give Lord St. Austell the third part of a handsome fortune, if indeed we are so fortunate as to find anything at all, which possibly we may not do."

"Well, let's find it first, and we can talk about Lord St. Austell afterwards. The finders of a big hoard are entitled to something, I suppose?"

"Very little. They may claim a trifling percentage, I believe, perhaps 2 per cent. or 3 per cent., on the value of the find as assessed by the Crown. Enough to pay the expenses of the journey to London to claim it. But even then, there are such pleasures in London, such wines, such lovely faces—a week's visit would be well worth all the trouble."

"Wines! I don't suppose the finest wine that ever was made would intoxicate me like a gallop over the hills here!" said Rees, doubtfully. "And as for faces, I don't believe there's another in England as handsome as Deborah's!"

An ugly flush rose in the elder man's cheeks at the mention of her name.

"Deborah! Why, she's a negress compared to the London girls. They are the pick of the beauty-basket, as I think you will say. For if you cannot judge a woman's beauty, who should, when all the pretty lasses in the county are waiting for you to throw them the handkerchief? But they are dumpy, dowdy creatures you will find when you get to London."

"And if we find all this, we shall only get a few pounds? But that is not fair. What right has the Crown to it, that never heard of it? Or Lord St. Austell, who laughed at the idea of its existence?"

"That's what I want to know. The Crown portion will perhaps be paid away in the pensions of those noblemen who are paid handsomely by the State for being the descendants of Charles the Second's mistresses. Or it may be spent in keeping up Buckingham Palace, where the Sovereign never lives, and where a collection of splendid pictures moulders away in the company of the Royal spiders, the public not being allowed to enter and see them. I don't know. And Lord St. Austell's portion? Well, he will be able to enjoy himself in town upon that," added Amos, with suggestive dryness.

"At any rate," said Rees with excitement, "the thing is first to find it, before we settle what's to be done with it."

"That is just what I say."

"How shall we begin?"

"You must take up a craze, say botany for instance, and start specimen-hunting inside the castle walls. You must have a pickaxe and spade; I will get you those up over the walls—and you must explore systematically, bit by bit. I will be on the watch outside. You will always let me know what part you are at work in, and I will keep watch. I have two hours in the middle of the day, and as many as you like at night."

"All right. We'll begin to-night."

They parted with only a few more words, for Rees was oppressed by the consciousness that, explain it away as he might, he was about to do an underhand action; and Goodhare, when he had gained a point, was not a man to weaken his effect by superfluous words.

That night the search began. Day after day and night after night it continued, and always without result, until the young man's heart grew sick within him, and the elder grew fierce with disappointed longing. In the hot afternoons, when the trees that grew thickly on the high banks of the Wye seemed to dance in a heat-mist; in the cool, summer nights, when the owls peered out with gleaming eyes from the ivy bushes which hung round the broken turrets, Rees worked on. He dug deep in the beaten earth which had collected in the ruined chambers. He clave with his pickaxe old beams that had fallen to the ground to become food for the busy worms. Not a grating in the ground that he did not examine; not a blocked-up doorway into which, by long and patient labor, he did not grope. Their way of working answered admirably. If any one from the neighborhood, or a party of tourists, approached the outer gate, Rees had instant warning from the watcher outside, and on the entrance of the visitors a handsome young man would be found seated on a broken step in the outer court or on a massive window embrasure in one of the damp, cool vaults below, attentively studying a bramble or a weed by the aid of a book or a microscope.

One curious discovery he made in the second week of his labors. It was that the earth on which the castle was built possessed the property of preserving, almost uninjured by damp or decay, anything which was buried at a certain depth within its bosom. For he came upon the bodies of various dead pets, a guinea-pig, a rabbit, and a white rat, to which his brothers, in their childhood, had given honorable sepulture within the castle walls; and they were all in a perfect state of preservation, except that they had become dry and shrivelled.

Amos Goodhare's information here came in to account for this. He had himself visited certain caves in the neighborhood of Bordeaux, in which the bodies of a dozen dead monks were preserved, their habits still clinging, uninjured, round the shrivelled and wasted forms. He gave Rees a scientific account of the properties of the soil which produced this effect, to which the young man was too much excited to take heed.

For he had got an idea into his head that the subterranean passage, if it existed at all, by which the unlucky Lord Hugh had tried to make his escape, must start from a certain large vaulted chamber, the base of which and part of the walls were formed in the rock itself. This chamber was the lowest part of the castle, and not being so much exposed as the rest to storm and siege, was in an excellent stage of preservation. It looked out through a deep-walled window over the river, which formed at this point a beautiful bend, with trees on one side and swelling meadow ground on the other. The original level of the floor was at present not easily to be found, as the rock surface was encumbered with stones and earth.

Here it was, however, that Rees had resolved to make a search, the thoroughness of which should be complete. At last, on the fifth evening of his labors, when he had dug deep down in the piled-up earth, until the last of the daylight had faded out of the sky, he felt the floor tremble under his feet.

He was by this time in utter darkness, his spade working mechanically in the hard earth.

He stopped, shivering from head to foot, cold from excitement and an instinct of mad joy. A hoarse shout escaped his lips in spite of himself.

The next moment it turned to a low-breathed exclamation of savage impatience. For a girl's voice called to him from the outer court, and in another minute the faint light which came through the doorway was blocked by her figure. It was Lady Marion Cenarth.

"What are you doing here, Rees Pennant," she asked sharply.

CHAPTER VII.

On hearing Lady Marion's voice, Rees felt his heart stand still. It was by this time quite dark in the cavernous chamber, so that he could only guess that she must have been watching, unseen by him, for an hour or more. He had a few moments to consider what he should do, for at the first sound of her voice he had stepped back hastily into the black shadow of one of the corners of the chamber, from whence he could observe her figure as long as she remained with her back to the faint light at the entrance.

"I know you are here, Rees. What are you doing?" she repeated.

And she passed with careful feet through the doorway, and began to advance towards the middle of the vaulted room.

Rees, interrupted thus, as he believed, on the brink of an important discovery, and afraid every moment that Lady Marion's feet would touch the iron grating he had just partly unearthed, felt that he could have killed her. But there was no time to be lost in explosions of resentment. The intruder had to be treated with, and at once. Throwing himself on his hands and knees, he crept hastily towards the doorway by which she had entered, while the slight noise he made in gliding over the rocky floor and the smooth-trodden earth which had in course of time accumulated over great part of it, was drowned by her own constant and excited calls to him by name. He slipped through the opening quickly, and ran up the rickety wooden steps which now connected these lower chambers of the ruins with those above.

A dozen steps more brought him to the open air, in the inner courtyard of the castle. Thence a little hazardous climbing enabled him to reach the outer wall, at a point immediately above the chamber in which he had been at work. Leaning over the ruined stonework so that his voice might penetrate through the embrasure of the great window below, he at last answered her repeated calls.

"Hallo!" he cried. "Hallo! Who's that down there? Is it you, Mrs. Crow? Do you want to shut up early to-night, eh?"

"It is I, Lady Marion Cenarth," answered a voice from the window below, tartly.

"You, Lady Marion, you!" cried Rees with well-acted astonishment. "Why, are you down in those dungeons? You'll catch your death of cold."

Rees would not have believed, ten minutes before, that he, the open-hearted, the recklessly sincere, could have assumed a sentiment he did not feel. But the hunger for hidden gold, the desire to keep his fancied discovery secret, had already done their work upon him.

"Can't you find your way out? Shall I come down and help you out?"

No answer at first. But she had evidently heard him, for her cries ceased. Rees climbed down much more slowly than he had come up, went to the top of the wooden steps, and called again.

"Lady Marion, Lady Marion, are you still there? Shall I come down and help you?"

She was stumbling towards him over the uneven floor. He leapt down and offered the assistance of his hand. There was only just light enough for her to see it, and for the first moment she refused haughtily, shrinking back as if the very offer had been an insult. The next, she characteristically tried to atone for this conduct by excessive humility, and seized his arm with pathetic eagerness. Rees, impatient and annoyed, helped her up the shaking steps without another word, while she muttered lame apologies for troubling him to come to her.

When they reached the open air, however, and she was able to see his face, the suspicions which had brought her to the castle returned in full force.

"Rees," she said, assuming an air of searching penetration, "it is of no use trying to deceive me. What makes you come here night after night? You do, I know, for I have just found it out from Mrs. Crow, and she says you never miss a single evening. And who is there about besides you? When I got down to that dungeon I distinctly heard somebody digging. The sound left off as soon as I called you, so I am certain there was some one."

"Really, Lady Marion, I don't think I am responsible for every noise heard in this old ruin, and don't know why I should be put through a long catechism about my movements here, when the place is free to every rat and bird in the country!"

In her usual blundering, tactless way the girl continued:

"The rats and birds only come to find a shelter. I don't see what a man should come here for late at night, unless he's a thief."

Of course this speech, according a little, as it did, with the feeling in his own conscience, maddened Rees.

"And, pray, is that the category in which you place me, your ladyship? Do you think I have formed a design for carrying off the castle, stone by stone, and building it up somewhere else?"

"No," answered she, "of course not. But how about the treasure lost in the Civil War?"

"Treasure!" echoed Rees, with a long, loud laugh of scornful amusement, which his intense excitement enabled him to simulate quite naturally. "Oh, if you believe that story, of course you can believe anything. If you were to hear I was a murderer, you would take it for granted. I think you will feel easier if I relieve you of my presence. It's not pleasant for a lady to be alone with a rogue so late in the evening."

He raised his cap, and was hurrying in the direction of the principal gate, and had reached the outer court of the castle, when Lady Marion, always weak when she ought to have been strong, ran after him in the humblest of moods.

"Rees! Rees!" she cried, "I didn't mean what I said. Come back! I'm going to Mrs. Crow for a candle, and I'm going to hunt through those rooms that we call the dungeons, for I'm sure I heard some one there. Won't you help me?"

Rees grew hot with fright. How on earth was he to keep her from carrying out this fatal intention? Unluckily for him, she noticed his hesitation, and putting a shrewd interpretation upon it, she ran on past him, and had burst open the door of the custodian's room before he could stop her.

Rees was beside himself. In his rage, impatience, and confusion, no plan for stopping her occurred to him, and he stood by the great gateway of the castle, kicking his heels against its huge beams in blank despair. As he did so, the gate, which alone was used now, creaked and slowly gave way behind him. He turned, and perceived that the big key of the gate had been left in the lock by Mrs. Crow when she admitted Lady Marion. He thrust it open, putting his shoulder against it impatiently, and found himself face to face with Amos Goodhare.

Rees uttered an exclamation of relief and joy. Here was advice and help.

"What am I to do?" he whispered hurriedly. "Lady Marion is here, suspects something, and insists on searching the place."

"Make up to her, of course," said Amos, who had very nearly added "you fool." "Let her think you are crazy about her, and she'll hold her tongue safe enough. Just the kind of girl—mad as a hatter and not too handsome; nothing like that sort to keep a man's secret. Go in."

Rees obeyed; indeed, Amos emphasized his injunction by a push which sent him staggering. But as the door was drawn softly to behind him, he felt his spirit rising in resentment at this change in the librarian's manner towards him. For Amos had suddenly dropped his pedantic respectfulness, his gentle movements, had looked at him with fierce impatience, and had been both rough and rude.

"I shall just wash my hands of the whole thing, and go home," he said to himself. But he hesitated, with his hand upon the gate. At that moment Lady Marion appeared at the door of the lodge, candle in hand, and with just a glance at him, made swiftly across the courtyard in the direction of the "dungeons," as the vaulted apartments overlooking the river were called.

"You needn't come with me, Mrs. Crow," he heard her call out as she ran. Rees followed her, all his anxiety about the safety of his secret alive again. She flew over the grass, a great sparrow-legged girl, not yet grown out of immature gawkiness, and got down the wooden steps somehow in a wonderfully short space of time. But in her haste she let the candle fall, and the light went out. Rees, at the top of the steps, looked down into the black vault, where he heard her groping about, and conceived the project of passing her again in the darkness, finding his way into the next and lower apartment, in which he had discovered the grating, and flattening down the earth to cover the traces of his work.

At the doorway, however, were two steps; stumbling on the damp and slippery surface of the second, he made enough noise for her to find him.

"Rees," she cried, "don't go away. This is a horrid place; something flapped past me. I feel quite frightened. It is you there, isn't it?"

Thinking that, by not answering, he should alarm her still more and induce her to find her way to the upper air, he was silent; and creeping away into a huge arched recess in the lower apartment, he leaned back and waited.

But Lady Marion, though susceptible to feminine fears, had some courage and more curiosity. She hunted about on her hands and knees in the outer room until she found her box of matches, struck one, discovered her candle, and relighting it, prepared for an exhaustive search.

He heard her manly footsteps—she and her sisters all wore flat-footed, "sensible" boots—tramping over the stones and the hard earth. He had just time to seize his pickaxe and spade, thrust them into a heap of loose rubble that filled one corner of the recess, and to kick a few spadefuls of earth over the uncovered grating, when she reappeared at the doorway.

Holding her candle high, she looked round the walls suspiciously, without condescending to take any notice of the young fellow's presence. Then she advanced slowly into the middle of the floor, peering curiously at the ground beneath her feet as she did so.

Rees held his breath. The next moment, making up his mind that there was nothing else to be done, he sprang forward and flung his arms around her.

"Marion, Marion," he cried, "it can't be true that you care for me if you won't so much as look at me."

The ruse succeeded. Lady Marion, who, in spite of her affectation of mannishness, was at heart rather a limp, pliable, and easily dominated young woman, was taken aback.

"Oh!" she exclaimed faintly, with a feeble feint of disengaging herself.

45

"I suppose you don't know—the earl won't have let you know—that I proposed to him for you, and that he rejected me almost as if I had been a groom."

"Don't, don't, Rees, I can't bear it. I've been miserable ever since."

"He told you then?"

"No, I guessed it from his manner, and when I found you didn't come to Llancader, and then I spoke to mamma, and she told me, and said it was no use hoping. Oh, but Rees, I don't think you can care as much as I do! You—you think more about getting this treasure than about me. I know you do. I know you were angry at my interrupting you. Yes, and I believe you *were* at work in here, and that it's only to prevent my finding out something that you are so nice to me now."

She thrust him away from her, noticed the roughness of the fresh-dug earth at her feet, and looked up at him with triumphant suspicion.

"Ah!" she cried in a whisper.

Rees was seized with a bold idea.

"Yes," he said, "I have been digging here; I have been trying to find the treasure. For if I could show him the way to a little fortune, the earl could scarcely refuse to let me marry you."

Lady Marion, fond of him as she was, had the sense to look doubtful.

"And Deborah? They say you like Deborah better than me!"

Rees was not past blushing, and he blushed now.

"Nonsense!" he said. "Look here, Marion."

Stooping down, he scraped away the loose earth and discovered the grating on which he had built such high hopes.

"This is what I found to-night," said he. "It may be only the covering of an old drain. But it may be something more. At any rate, that is my secret, which I have confided to nobody but you. Is that confidence enough? Now do you believe I care for you?"

It was a bold stroke, and he watched the effect in desperate excitement. Lady Marion's sallow face lighted up with eagerness as great as his own as she looked down at the rusty grating, which, slightly displaced during Rees's labours, shook under the tread.

"But did you do it for me, Rees—really for me?" she asked still half-doubtfully.

"If I had not, why should I confide in you? I did not want you to know my aims yet, certainly; I was too much humiliated by your father. But you have found me out, so you may as well know everything. Now, Marion, if ever I get your father to accept me for a son-in-law, will you have me?"

The poor affectionate girl was overjoyed. She hung about him, kissed his hands and his hair, and assured him that she would wait ten years for him if a prince were to woo her. She begged him to see her home as far as the park gates, as a compensation for the fact that they would have to be circumspect and content to see each other seldom. It was Rees who, impatient at her demonstrativeness, impressed this upon her.

"But I can come and see you at the same place to-morrow evening," said she. "Mademoiselle de Laval always leaves us quite undisturbed in the evening, and thinks we are busy over our Greek. I can slip out without the least danger. I shall come; don't be afraid."

Rees was already wishing her or himself at the bottom of the sea. Overwhelmed with shame and anger at his own conduct, he bade her as hasty a farewell as she would allow, returning her passionate kisses with embraces so reluctant and perfunctory that if she had not been so infatuated they must have chilled her own warmth.

Then, when she had left him and disappeared through a little side-gate into the park, he crept, with slow feet and hanging head, towards Goodhare's lodging.

The librarian was enjoying a frugal supper of a couple of poached eggs, a slice of bread and butter, and a glass of milk; and as he ate he studied a heavy, much-used volume of Cicero.

The young man shut up the book impetuously and flung himself into a chair opposite to Amos.

"I've found the entrance to the passage, I believe," said he, "a wide grating under two feet of earth, with a couple of stone steps to be seen underneath."

Amos started up with an exclamation of triumph.

"And I ought to be able to take full advantage of it, for I'm on my way to become a very finished scoundrel."

He related the incidents of his discovery and of his interview with Lady Marion. Goodhare listened with the ugly look of covetousness in his eyes which had sometimes shocked Rees before now. When he had finished, Amos burst out into a laugh of hideous, satyr-like raillery.

"Don't pretend to be ashamed of your conquest; that sort of modesty doesn't deceive me. And I won't distress you by asking for any details of the interview."

Rees started up, his face flushed, his hair disordered, his whole bearing speaking of shame for himself, but also of indignation against his companion.

"You are making me a thief, Amos; you are making me a rascal; but you have not yet made me forget that I was born a gentleman," said he.

The next moment, Amos meanwhile going on quietly with his poached eggs and bread and butter, the poor lad seemed to realize what an empty boast it was that he had uttered so proudly, and he sank down again in his chair and buried his face in his hands. But the fascination of the hidden treasure soon came over him again, driving out all other thoughts and feelings. Springing up once more, and leaning across the table to make his words more emphatic, he whispered:

"Goodhare, it's all up with us. I left the grating exposed, and forgot to fill up the hole in the earth above it!"

Amos had the wit to hide part of what he felt; but he betrayed enough to show Rees a little more of the demoniacal side of his character.

The two men parted that night with hearts and minds burdened with the deepest anxiety. The poking about with a stick of a couple of Mrs. Crow's children might reveal enough to set the neighborhood talking and prying, and then good-bye to visions of a golden independence.

CHAPTER VIII.

On the following morning Amos Goodhare, for the first time since his dismissal, visited Llancader Castle. He asked modestly whether he could see Mademoiselle de Laval, having, from his knowledge of the habits of the place, been able to choose the hour when she was resting in her own sitting-room before beginning the day's labors.

He was shown up to this apartment, where the lady received him very graciously. Amos took care to let her think that his visit was prompted by an overwhelming wish to know whether the recent damp weather had affected her rheumatism, and it was not until he had listened sympathetically to an exhaustive list of her "symptoms," that he enquired after the family. Then he asked, confidentially, whether there was any truth in a report he had heard that Lady Marion was engaged to the eldest son of the late Captain Pennant. To this, Mademoiselle de Laval replied with horror on her face that the very mention of his name was forbidden in the household.

Amos Goodhare's face immediately underwent a change, and expressed the deepest anxiety. In answer to her questions he then very reluctantly confessed that Lady Marion and Rees Pennant were in the habit of meeting late in the evening. Mademoiselle was much alarmed, but at first inclined to be incredulous.

"Very well," said Amos quietly. "I would not take the trouble to prove what I say if I did not feel so much admiration for you and so much grateful interest in his lordship's family. But find out whether Lady Marion was in the house last night between eight and nine. What would happen to you if anything were to go wrong with one of the young ladies? It goes to my heart to think of the cruel injustice which might be done to a lady of such talents and accomplishments as yourself."

He did not prolong the interview after that; for he had succeeded in thoroughly alarming her, and he felt sure that in future Rees would be able to pursue his researches without interruption from Lady Marion.

Rees went to the old castle very early that morning. It was a pouring wet day, and he had to tell the custodian that he had left something in the ruins the evening before in order to account for his appearance there in weather which no sane person, without some strong reason, would have chosen for a ramble among the mouldering stones.

Breathless with anxiety, he crossed the two courts, and entered the vault with streams of water pouring down his mackintosh. The rain had done him good service; not only had it prevented Mrs. Crow's boys from wandering among the ruins, but it washed down in torrents from the upper chambers, and rushing through the exposed grating, carried with it a quantity of the earth which had accumulated above. Rees could see the stone steps underneath, and with fiery energy he dug away spadeful after spadeful, until at last the grating, loosened in its place, shook under his feet. A few more frenzied efforts, and he was able to raise it half a dozen inches. He could scarcely restrain a cry of joy, which, however, speedily changed to a groan of disappointment.

The grating was kept down by no hinges; it was more than two feet wide, of clumsy, old-fashioned workmanship, though of much later date than the last rebuilding of the castle in the fourteenth century. With great difficulty Rees raised it, tearing the flesh off his hands as he did so on the iron bars, which were caked with a hard deposit of rust. He had taken the precaution of bringing in his pocket a candle and matches. Striking a light he descended about a dozen rough and much worn stone steps in a sort of well hewn out of the solid rock. He had to move very carefully, as the steps were steep and unevenly covered with earth which the late rains had converted into mud; while the rude walls were too slimy with damp for the irregularities of their surface to afford him any hold.

The air down here was cold; it chilled his heated body and made his teeth chatter. Taking a couple of steps rather more quickly than the rest in his excitement and impatience, his right foot suddenly splashed into water. Drawing it back hastily, he peered into the darkness at his feet, and saw that what he had taken for the entrance to a subterranean passage was apparently nothing more nor less than an old, long disused well.

With a moan of anger and bitter disappointment, he sat down, with his feet on the lowest dry step, while a cold perspiration made him shiver from head to foot, and at the same time his forehead burned, and his mouth was so parched that, as he drew breath, he emitted a choking cough. He felt as if the hidden gold had been wrenched out of his eagerly clutching fingers, the gold which was to have supported his mother, showered presents on Deborah, restored his prestige as the genius of his family, and perhaps made him an earl's son-in-law—for somehow that first idea of making known the discovery to the earl had, under the fire of Goodhare's discourses, melted quite away.

He had brought his spade with him, and he sat holding it idly in his hand, and not heeding the fact that the rain-water from above was all the while trickling down the steps, making his seat not only damp but dangerous. Suddenly he slipped, and the spade in his hand scraped the ground at the bottom of the water.

It could not be very deep then! Perhaps it was not a well at all!

His excitement returning, he drew the spade slowly and carefully from left to right, stirring the foul mud at the bottom of the stagnant water, and causing noxious odours to rise from it. The water was not more than a foot and a half deep. The evil smells were so overpowering that he felt himself turn sick, and had to go back up a half a dozen steps to get fresh air and to recover himself.

When he redescended he found that the water had gone down a little. At first he thought this might only be his fancy, so by the faint light of his dwindling candle-end he watched. Surely enough, the water-line on the shiny wall seemed to emerge higher and higher above the foul black liquid, and Rees could hear the quick drip drip of water below him. Again he sounded with his spade even more carefully than before. Close under the bottom step one corner of the implement got caught in a hole, which proved to be round and about seven inches in diameter. As Rees passed the spade backwards and forwards, he heard a rushing sound, and the water began to go down much more rapidly. This small hole, he thought, must be the top of a drain-pipe which had become choked with obstacles which the spade removed.

He glanced at his candle—there was not half an inch of it left. Would that water never go down? With frantic impatience he dragged his spade to and fro from wall to wall. Work as hard as he would, he had not time. The candle-end, which he held in his left hand and glanced at anxiously, grew hot between his fingers; then the wick fell over, burning him so that he had to shake it off hastily on to the wet step, where it went out with a faint little hiss and splutter.

"Hang it!" almost shouted Rees, forgetting his caution, forgetting everything in his frantic impatience.

"Hallo!" cried a voice above, which sounded hollow in the rocky cavity.

Rees could have bitten his tongue out. He leaned against the uneven and slippery wall, shivering with alarm and disappointment. Had he fatally betrayed himself? Who was the intruder? All that he could tell as yet was that it was the voice of a young man. Rees kept quite still and silent, hoping against hope that the man would not see the opening in the floor of the vaulted chamber. The day was so dark that this was just possible. But the hope was vain. Rees heard footsteps, and then another exclamation as the tiny light of a match appeared for a few moments at the opening in the floor above him and then went out.

At that moment his foot slipped, making a slight noise.

"Who's there?" cried the voice above. "Not Rees, not Rees Pennant? For God's sake, answer?"

Rees recognised the voice by this time. It was that of Sep Jocelyn, one of his most devoted admirers and friends.

This Sep was a short and rather thick-set fair man, without hair on his face, who was five-and-thirty, but looked ten years younger until you examined quite closely the little thread-like wrinkles which crossed and recrossed his face in all directions, and the white streaks in his thick fair hair. While still very young, he had been left an orphan with command of money; as usual in such cases, he had been ruined in character and fortune in the most commonplace way—by bad women, worse men, and drink. At three-and-thirty he had been discovered in abject circumstances by an old aunt, the widow of an admiral, who had carried him off with her to her house in Carstow, where she could still keep up some show of state on an extremely limited income.

Here she tried hard to regenerate him, and as far as that could be done, she succeeded. That is to say, he became entirely respectable, lived soberly, went to church, and was a most submissive, affectionate, and good-humored companion to his aunt, of pleasant, if somewhat effeminate manners. But at heart he was blasé and cynical, with a surprised feeling that any one could be so misguided as to bestow on him so much attention and kindness, which he certainly was not worth. And yet he was grateful, in a certain way, making due allowance for the facts that his aunt had wanted a companion, and that she belonged to the sex which has a fondness for the reclamation of ne'er-do-weels. Belonging to that class of men who, incapable of leading, have an instinct of attaching themselves where they will be led, he had become the devoted satellite of Rees Pennant, whose handsome face and dashing manner fascinated and enchained him.

Rees, who made the not unnatural mistake of rating Sep's devotion higher than it was worth, felt intensely relieved on learning who his discoverer was. In an instant he made up his mind to confide in him. Knowing, as he did, that he must have help to prosecute his researches further, it seemed, indeed, that no better assistant could be obtained.

"S-h!" he hissed, and creeping up three or four of the rough steps as quickly and quietly as he could, he asked in an eager whisper, "Who is with you?"

"Little Jack, Mrs. Crow's boy. He's outside. I told him not to come down; the room above us is ankle deep in mud. What are you doing down there? What a pickle you're in!"

"I'm clean to what I shall be before I've done," said he, in a low voice, as he crept up the remaining steps, replaced the grating with Sep's help, and taking off his waistcoat, laid it upon the bars and shovelled a layer of earth on to it.

Then, silencing all his companion's questions until they should be above ground, he seized his arm and hurried him upstairs, where they found little Jack making mud-pies in the outer doorway. In a few words, and with an air of the deepest confidence, Rees then told Sep the story of the MS., the supposed lost treasure, of his discoveries and his hopes. Sep was desperately interested, ready to hazard his own limbs, if needful, to help his friend's researches, although he knew by this confidence Rees was only making a virtue of necessity.

They decided that, as Sep had not the same right of entry as Rees, some way must be found to draw him up over the castle walls. Sep, who, on hearing his friend had gone into the castle, had braved torrents of rain and huge stretches of mud to meet him, was ready to submit even to this.

They left the ruins together, and meeting Goodhare, who was, as usual, on the watch outside, Rees introduced him as a confidant, and related his discoveries. Amos could scarcely conceal his rage and disappointment—rage that a new hand should be engaged in the work, to take his share of the hoped-for spoil; disappointment at the result of the discovery on which Rees counted so much.

"What on earth possesses you, Pennant, to imagine that any good can come of your finding an old blocked-up drain?" he asked scornfully.

Rees, exhausted by excitement and manual labour of an unaccustomed kind, and flushed by a sense of achievement, was incensed by the question and by this familiar manner of address.

"The feeling which possesses me," he answered promptly, "is indignation that I should associate myself in any work with an impudent and lazy rascal, who waits outside for the result of other people's labor."

Instead of resenting this insolence, Goodhare listened with his head bent down, as if with remorse, and made full and ample apology for his impatience.

But when he had turned to go back to his library, after a most affectionate and respectful farewell to Rees, and a cordial one to the new associate in the enterprise, Sep linked his arm within that of his friend, and suggested, in his mincing voice and manner:

"I say, Rees, you made a mistake with that old boy just now. You didn't notice his face as he hung his head down. Now, if you were to call me a humbug, a liar, and a thief, I should forget it, knowing that we're friends for all that. But this old fox remembers. I know he hates me, but through thick and thin I'm going to treat him like a brother."

"Well, I don't pretend I can hide my feelings," said Rees, in a tone of large generosity.

"It's necessary, though, when one's not quite acting on the square."

"What do you mean, Sep?" and Rees turned on him quite fiercely. "Do you think I'm such a skunk as not to give Lord St. Austell what belongs to him, shamefully as he has treated me?"

"Oh, no, no, Rees, I forgot for the moment," answered Sep.

And he looked up into his friend's handsome face with amused curiosity. Did Rees really believe in his own integrity still?

CHAPTER IX.

THE rain continued to fall in torrents all day long after Rees Pennant's discovery of the mysterious drain. He took Sep Jocelyn home with him, and they waited in fiery impatience for the evening, unable to settle to any occupation or amusement but that of speculating on the marvels they might find. Godwin was away; Hervey was reading in his own room; Deborah was, if the truth must be known, cooking in the kitchen before dinner, brushing Rees's macintosh afterwards. The only person, therefore, who interfered with their excited *tête à tête* was Mrs. Pennant, who noticed her darling son's restlessness, and was curious as to the cause.

"Well, my little mother," said Rees, throwing his arms around her and giving her a more affectionate hug than he had bestowed upon her of late, "and supposing I tell you that I see a prospect of helping you, of doing more for you than either Godwin the grumpy or Hervey the heroic! What would you say then, mother?"

"My dear boy, I should only say that you were doing what I always expected of you," said she, too much delighted by this welcome change in his manner towards her to be very curious as to the precise meaning of these large promises.

"And without becoming any man's servant, either," continued Rees, whose strong point was not prudence.

Sep twitched his friend's sleeve warningly unseen by Mrs. Pennant.

"Rees only means," he put in with his quiet little mincing voice, "that he thinks he has a chance of a berth in London at a good salary."

"Yes, yes; in London, that's it," assented Rees quickly.

"In London," cried Mrs. Pennant. "Oh, I should like to live in London again; nothing would please me better."

Rees and Sep both grew suddenly subdued and reticent.

"I—I don't know whether that could be managed, mother dear, until my position was more secure. You see I—I—in fact, I'm not sure at all about it yet, you know."

"I don't want to force your confidence, my son, since I see there is some little surprise intended for me. But if it is any situation which depends on talent and a good appearance," she went on proudly, "I have no fear for you."

Rees turned the subject in a tremulous voice. He loved his mother, and thought of her continually throughout this enterprise, now congratulating himself that he might be able to support her in the comfort and luxury which he considered to be the only suitable surrounding for her, now trying to stifle the knowledge that she would look upon this secret search with the most violent disapproval.

So he took Sep off to the stable-yard to hunt for a second spade, a piece of rope, and for an old lantern which Rees knew to be lying about there. They found it, rubbed it up, and put a piece of candle in it. Unfortunately, one of the glass sides was broken, but they thought that this would not matter.

At tea, Rees was preternaturally gay, Sep unusually silent. Soon afterwards, on pretence of going to Mrs. Kemp's, they left the drawing-room; and taking with them the spade, the rope, and the lantern, slipped through a little door in the wall at the bottom of the garden, and made for the ruins.

It was unusually dark, for the grey clouds were thick in the sky and the rain was still falling. Outside the castle walls, under the trees on the west side, Amos Goodhare, a gaunt figure shivering in the damp, was waiting. Very few words were exchanged between them, for their plan of action was already settled. Then Rees left the other two, and going round to the castle gates, pulled the bell which summoned the custodian.

Mrs. Crow was rather cross, not having expected to be disturbed so late.

"Really, Master Rees," she said, using, as most people did, his boyish name, "I can't think what you're up to, a-wandering about them ruins at all hours of the day and night. And if it's to meet Lady Marion, who came in here after you last night, I can tell you I'll not be a party to it, that I won't."

"My dear old soul," said Rees, throwing his arm round her in his fascinatingly affectionate way, "there's nothing I want less than to have Lady Marion always at my heels. So, if she turns up while I'm inside, you just tell her I'm not there. Why, I come here so that I may study in peace away from the girls, they pester one so."

And, with a light air of all-conqueror, he tossed up into the air a book which he had taken care to bring as evidence of his veracity.

Mrs. Crow shook her head and began to chuckle indulgently.

"Oh, what a lad you are, with your carneying ways. I suppose it's poor Miss Deborah you mean, since everybody knows she's dying for ye. Well, well, some hearts are made to be broken, and others made to break them, I suppose. But it's a pity, for sure, that you don't make it up together, for you'd make a handsome couple!"

Rees laughed, and passed in not ill-pleased. His was not a nature with any great depth of passion to bestow on any woman. But he knew that Deborah was the handsomest and altogether the nicest girl in the neighborhood. So it pleased him to hear that she was in love with him. In his way, too, he loved her, and would most probably have proposed to her on his father's death but for the influences which had lately been brought to bear upon him. At present, however, no woman held any but the most insignificant place in his heart or mind, and as he hurried to the vaulted chamber all thought of Deborah went out of his head.

Everything was secure. After one glance in the dusk, he returned to the inner court, and climbing to the outer western wall of the castle by the help of a broken turret staircase and the branches of one of the trees which had sprung up in what once were rooms, he leaned over the broken battlements and whistled softly. The trees grew tall and thick outside the walls on this side, and the ivy clung to the ruins with the strong clasp of a couple of centuries. Amid the mass of foliage Rees could not for several minutes distinguish the two men's figures in the obscurity far below him, though he could hear their voices softly answering him.

Assured that all was safe, and that they were ready, he made one end of the rope he carried fast to one of the iron bars used in the building of the castle, which time and weather had laid bare, and threw the other end over the wall.

"All right!" said Sep's voice in a husky whisper.

The strong, gnarled branches of the ivy afforded such a firm support to the feet that Sep, who, like most ne'er-do-weels, had had a short spell of the sea, found no difficulty in climbing up, by the aid of the rope, very quickly.

Then they hissed out "All right!" to Amos, watching below, and taking the rope with them descended to the scene of their search.

"Why doesn't Goodhare come too?" asked Rees, in a low voice. "He could get up quite as well as you, and we shall want all the help we can."

Sep uttered his mincing little laugh.

"Because our friend prefers leaving the risk to us, and doesn't consider that sharing terms need begin until the profits roll in," said he.

Sep had the blessing of shrewdness and the curse of never being able to profit by it.

"What risk?"

"The risk of being found out, and the risk of losing our limbs or our lives. If Lord Hugh really did lose his life down there, you know, why shouldn't we?"

"And supposing you and I choose to say—'No risk, no profit'?"

"Then he would choose to tell the earl all about it, and you and I would look very small."

Rees walked on in silence. He was beginning to see some of the disadvantages of having a rogue for a partner. At sight of the grating, however, when they had removed the covering, everything but the excitement of the search went out of his head. Not heeding Sep's admonitions to be careful, he lighted the lantern, and went down the steps with so much haste that at the bottom he slipped, and found himself sitting in the mud on the floor of the little chamber, close to the mouth of the drain-pipe.

Luckily, all the water had by this time drained off down the pipe, and he was able to make a thorough examination of the walls and floor. The little chamber was about six feet square, rough-hewn in the rock. The walls were wet and slimy, and the floor was deep in malodorous mud. As he slipped into the slush, his heels fell with a dull thud on something which was not rock. Not heeding the mud, nor the whispered cries of his friend above, who was afraid he had hurt himself, Rees groped about with his hands in the slime which covered the floor.

Suddenly Sep was startled by a wild cry. Half beside himself with fear for his companion, he began to descend the steps himself. He saw the light of the lantern moving about below him; the worst had not happened therefore: Rees was alive. As he put his foot on the bottom step, Sep found himself suddenly seized by a strange figure with wild eyes and face bespattered with mud, coated from head to foot with slime. Being a particularly neat and dapper little man in his appearance, Sep rather resented this embrace.

"I've found something!" stammered Rees hoarsely.

"Yes, I see you have; and you may keep it, and welcome," answered Sep, trying ruefully to brush the mud off his own coat-sleeves.

"But listen, Sep, listen, you don't understand," went on Rees, at a white heat of excitement. "I've found a trap-door in the floor. What do you think of that?"

"Perhaps it's another drain," suggested Sep, who was inclined to be sceptical about the whole business, knowing by experience that fortunes are more easily lost than found.

"Nonsense! We've got to open it. Hold the lantern and give me the spade."

Sep obeyed, and stood on the bottom step, a pitiful figure, holding the lantern aloft while he shivered with the damp, grew sick with the smells, and gazed at his coat-sleeves with ever-increasing annoyance to think that he had let himself be drawn into such a crack-brained enterprise.

Meanwhile, Rees, with feverish energy, was cleaning the mud in spadefuls from a space on the floor about two feet square. When this was done, down he went on his knees again, and after several futile efforts, lifted, not a trap-door, but a heavy square piece of wood, like a box lid, which had evidently been sawn out of the trunk of a tree in the roughest manner, and chopped into an uneven square. This was about five inches thick. When it was dragged away, the light of the lantern showed an abyss of blackness underneath, at which both men instinctively drew back a little. After a few seconds, Rees knelt down again beside the hole and peered into it with keen eyes.

"There are steps down cut into the rock, Sep," he whispered at last hoarsely. "Quite straight down they are, only just notches for the feet," he went on. "And there's an iron rail fixed close to the wall at the side of them, like those in locks on a river."

Sep stooped gingerly, and looked down too.

"Stand back," said Rees impatiently, "I'm going down."

But Sep, one of whose qualities was an absolutely unselfish power of self-sacrifice, prevented him.

"Don't be absurd, Rees," he said quietly. "I can climb better than you, and it may come to be a climbing matter. Give me the lantern."

He took it from his companion's unwilling hand, and began the descent. But when he had gone ten or twelve steps it seemed to Rees that the lantern swung from side to side, and that Sep was going down very slowly.

"Are you all right, old man?" he asked anxiously.

No answer. At that moment the light in the lantern went suddenly out, and there came up to his ears a dull sound like the fall of some heavy body.

"Sep, Sep, are you all right?" again he shouted, in a voice that rang in the hollow space.

Again no answer. The truth flashed upon him. The cavernous abyss below him was full of foul poisonous gases, such as he had often heard of at the bottom of old wells. There was not a moment to lose. Already poor Sep, stupefied by the noxious vapors, might be beyond the reach of help. Fastening the rope they had brought with them to the top of the perpendicular iron railing in such a manner that the knots, wedged in on the top step, kept it firm, he fastened the other end round his waist, and half-climbed, half-slid down into the blackness below.

He had not gone down far, however, before he began to feel the influence of the vapors which had overcome his friend. He found himself growing giddy, and then for a moment, which seemed to him an hour, he partly lost consciousness of what he was doing. But he struggled with this creeping paralysis, and by a strong effort of will recovered command of himself and remembered his errand. The length of the rope just enabled him to get to the bottom of the steps. The darkness was absolute. He held his breath to avoid inhaling any more of the foul, heavy air than he could help, and, stooping down with outstretched hands, touched the insensible body of his friend. He gathered him up with the support of the rope, and being lucky enough to find the iron handrail at once, he dragged himself and Sep up the rugged steps as quickly as the heavy burden would permit.

59

Rees's movements had been so rapid that the whole proceeding of descent and ascent had not occupied more than a minute. Short as the time was, however, it had been long enough for the poisonous gas to take effect. By the time they got to the little chamber which contained the opening of the drain, Rees felt that he was succumbing to its influence, and that the only chance, not only for Sep, but for himself, lay in reaching the purer air above. He staggered across the muddy floor, and with efforts which grew every moment more frantic as again he felt a dizziness like approaching death come over him, he dragged his companion, whether dead or alive he did not know, up—up to the floor of the vaulted room.

"Thank God! thank God!" he cried deliriously; and then he turned, thinking the voice was that of some one else.

Then again for an instant he remembered where he was, and staggering about on the rocky floor, called, "Where are you, Sep?" in a husky, weak whisper. He felt his limbs give way under him, and, sinking on the floor, he had just strength left to reach his friend's motionless body, when his senses left him.

CHAPTER X.

SEP was the first to recover consciousness. Little by little, beginning by half-opening his eyes in the darkness only to shut them again, without thought, without memory, he at last woke with a start to the knowledge that he was lying on something very hard, in a cold, dark place, that his teeth were chattering, and that he was very badly bruised on his right arm and side. Then, turning, he saw the pale remains of the daylight, or the pale beginnings of the moonlight, coming through the deep embrasure of the window. Following the line of faint light with eyes in which the intelligence was scarcely yet awake, he saw on the floor, almost close to him, what looked like a tumbled heap of dark clothes.

Then he remembered. Shaking off the stupor, which again seemed to be overpowering him, Sep turned his friend's body so that he could dimly see the face. At first he thought he was dead, and with a shriek of horror Sep started to his feet. But Rees stirred at the sound, and in a moment his friend was again beside him, loosening his clothes, watching eagerly the first faint signs of returning life, and muttering curses on his own weakness in having helped him in this dangerous, mad enterprise. At last Rees, after uttering a few faint sighs, rolled over on his left side, and again his companion thought he was dying, if not dead.

Springing up again with a despairing exclamation, Sep was on the point of risking discovery by rushing to the lodge to summon help, when Rees, as if instinctively knowing that his project was in danger, recovered himself quite suddenly, like a child waking out of sleep, and stopped him with a hoarse cry.

"Where is it? What have you done with it, Sep?" he asked wildly, but in a weak voice.

"Done with what?" asked Sep, startled by his friend's tone, and fancying at first that the incidents of the night, whatever they might have been, had turned his brain.

"The gold! You know," said Rees mysteriously.

Sep sat down beside him, much excited.

"Gold. Did you really find any, Rees? Tell me just what happened. I only remember feeling giddy and then drowsy, and then the light went out."

"You fell down, and I went to bring you up. You were right deep down there, on the ground, insensible. I couldn't see you, but I felt you, and I dragged you up. And then I saw gold, gold, shining all round us on the walls in the darkness; but when I touched it I found it all like dry powder. I suppose I was dreaming, Sep," he added slowly.

"Of course you were. And you went down to pull me up?" Sep went on wonderingly. "It was very silly; you might have been overcome just as I was, and then we should have lain dead together."

"Well, that would be much better than for people to say Rees Pennant left his friend to die alone."

This sort of romantic outburst became Rees, because a little Welsh rhodomontade was natural to him; and, indeed, he was physically brave enough. Sep took his hand affectionately.

"Now, Rees," said he, "we must get away, and never come near this villainous pest-hole again."

Rees pushed his friend's hand away like an impatient boy.

"You need not come again," he said. "But I shall come here again and again, and go down that hole again and again, until I find what it leads to, and whether there is anything in it worth finding."

He spoke with dogged obstinacy, but indeed after the evening's adventures, and the cold awakening from that dream of gold which turned at the touch, there only remained to him the embers of hope and sullen persistency in carrying this project through to the end.

"Oh, well, then, of course if you come, I shall," said Sep, in his little chirpy voice. "We'll come, and come as long as you like, till we both find a fool's grave down there."

Rees did not answer. He was busy replacing the grating over the hole, and covering it up as before. Then they walked in silence, still suffering from a sort of lightness in the head, out into the open air, and climbed up to the spot on the wall where Sep had been drawn up. By the same means he was now let down again very silently, by the watery light of a moon that was battling not very successfully with the clouds. Then Rees walked out by the gate, as he could do without summoning Mrs. Crow, and rejoined the other two men under the castle wall.

Amos Goodhare was in a state of much excitement, and professed great enthusiasm over the devotion which each of the young men had displayed towards the other.

"It is such hazardous enterprises as these," he said warmly, "which bring out in their brightest colors the qualities of young men."

"Yes, and of older ones too," assented Sep, in his best fool's manner, which the librarian did not yet understand.

Goodhare heartily applauded Rees's determination to go through with the adventure, but declined the offer that he should share the dangers of the next descent with a good-humored laugh.

"I am too old," he said. "My limbs are too stiff for such doings. What would have become of me if I had been in the place of either of you? If in Sep Jocelyn's, I should have been too heavy for you to lift; if in yours, I should not have been active enough to get him out in time. No, I must take the humbler part of watcher, and be content therefore with such share of the spoils—if there are to be any spoils—as you think due to my initiative."

The younger men could not but agree with the justice of this reasoning, in whatever light they might consider these last words. They parted for the night very soon, Rees declaring that he had a plan, and that if Sep would be at the same place under the walls on the next evening but one, he would by that time, he thought, be in a position to perform the perilous adventure in safety.

On the evening appointed, therefore, Rees, without increasing the risk of exciting suspicion by meeting the other two men first, passed as usual through the castle gates and mounted to his place on the west wall. The weather was fine and mild, so that they had to wait their opportunity of escaping the eyes of such of the townsfolk as had strolled this way for a summer evening's ramble. Sep's seafaring experiences now stood him in good stead. As soon as Amos, on the watch a few yards below in the cricket meadow, gave the signal that no one was near, Sep seized the rope, which was almost hidden by the thick ivy, and was safe on the top of the wall in a few seconds.

Then came a more severe trial for their patience. Rees and his companion had scarcely got down to the inner court of the castle when they saw in the distance a small party of young tradesmen of the town and their lasses, who were being escorted over the ruins by one of Mrs. Crow's sons. The two young men, knowing every corner of the old building, easily found a hiding-place for Sep and for a mysterious parcel which Rees had brought, hidden under his rug. This rug he now quickly spread on the remains of one of the wide inner walls, and throwing himself upon it, he lit a cigarette and opened before him a book, on which he appeared to be intent as the excursion party came up. He had to look up then, however, for he and his family were so popular that more than one of the intruders stopped to make kind and respectful inquiries after his mother, which Rees, though boiling with impatience to get rid of them, was obliged to answer civilly. This incident caused a delay of nearly an hour before the two young men could begin their work.

At last, however, the wicket-gate swung to behind the party. Sep instantly, on a whistle from Rees, came out of his hiding-place, and they descended together to the vaulted room. Here Rees, going down on his knees on the floor, opened his mysterious parcel and spread out before Sep's inquiring eyes a great coil of old garden hose, neatly repaired in various places, and furnished at one end with a sort of macintosh bag.

"What's that for?" asked Sep.

"To breathe through," answered Rees in a tone of triumph. "It was the foul air that put out the light and overcame you and me. To go down there safely one must have air from above, like a diver. I've stopped up all the holes in the tubing myself, and I've joined our own garden hose with Mr. Long's, which I borrowed out of his tool-shed without troubling him for permission; and I've contrived, as you see, a sort of loose air-tight mask at one end to cover the nostrils as well as the mouth. Provided with this, I believe I can breathe down there as freely as up here. Anyhow, I mean to try."

Sep, though not inclined to put much faith in this ingenious arrangement, and, in fact, most dismally minded concerning their chances of escaping with their lives out of the adventure, listened submissively to all his friend's instructions, and agreed at last, with much reluctance, to be the one left at the top, while Rees was to test his own apparatus.

Rees then showed his friend an old miner's lantern which he had bought secondhand in Cardiff years ago when he was a boy. A very long rope completed his equipment. One end of this rope he tied round his waist, fastening the other securely to the bars of the iron grating; then attaching the air-tight mask over his face, with the tube depending from it, he took the lantern in his hand and began the descent.

Sep's office was to keep the tubing straight, that the supply of air might be unimpeded; also to watch the rope, and, when he saw it jerked three times, to help his friend's return to the upper air by hauling it up with all his might.

Although he had made light of the risks he was about to run in order to encourage his friend, Rees was really quite as fully aware of the desperate nature of his enterprise as Sep was. All definite hopes about the supposed treasure had, indeed, given place in his mind to the mere desire to carry on to the end an exciting adventure; for Rees, though deficient in moral strength, had just the needful dash and daring for a dangerous feat of this kind. He thought he saw in the discovery of these underground steps, not the confirmation of Goodhare's ambitious hopes, but the foundation for them. It was, therefore, as an explorer rather than as a robber that he made this third descent.

His lantern, meanwhile, was certainly growing very dim. He had done everything so rapidly that only a few seconds had elapsed since he had began the descent. He now ran down the slope, but stopped short just in time, with a guttural ejaculation of horror.

For the rock ended abruptly in a perpendicular cliff.

Rees, shaking and shivering with an odd feeling of having been very near the Great End, peered down. He could see nothing. There was a cavernous depth of blackness below, but he could tell neither its width nor its height, for his light was waning rapidly. Suddenly he caught sight of something which roused him again to a frantic pitch of do-all, dare-all curiosity. It was a rope attached to an iron staple at his feet, and hanging down. The temptation to go further was now irresistible. Throwing himself first into a sitting position, with his legs hanging over the rock, he tried the rope, giving it a tug with his disengaged hand. It seemed firm. That decided him. He fastened his lantern to the rope which was tied round his waist, and seizing the other, swung himself over and began descending, hand under hand. He had not gone down more than a couple of yards, however, when the rope, which was old and rotten, gave way, and he was thrown to the ground. Luckily, this was only a couple of feet or so below him, and he picked himself up at once, unhurt, with his lantern unextinguished.

As he did so, he noticed a strange sound like heavy hailstones falling. Beginning as he touched the ground, it continued for a few moments after, growing gradually fainter. This, he found, proceeded from the walls, which were here only just far enough apart to allow him to pass without touching them. The disturbance he made in the still air had caused hundreds of little flat flakes of stone to crumble off the rocky sides and to fall to the ground.

He was now, he felt sure, going under the river; for the passage went straight forward without slope or curve. He was conscious, as he hurried on, of a strange acrid smell, quite unlike the damp heavy fumes which, in spite of his precautions, had faintly reached his nostrils in the stage above. Here it was dry—strangely dry—with an atmosphere which, although not hot, seemed to parch the flesh as he passed.

But, in the meantime, breathing through the tube was becoming difficult, and a mad impatience seized him when he found that there was a sudden turn in the passage just in front of him, while he had come so close to the end of the tubing that the length left would not allow him to pass the corner. If he went carefully, however, he thought he could, by the last rays of his dying candle, manage to look round.

Very cautiously he now moved; two steps more; yes, he could just do it. The tube was stretched to its utmost length; already he felt himself half suffocated, as if it had caught on something. But as he reached the corner, and held the little flickering light up to see what it led to, his eyes fell on a sight which would have stopped his breath with horror even if he had been breathing free air.

Seated on a chest against the wall, leaning his head back, and meeting Rees Pennant's stare of dismay with eyes wide open and horror-struck as his own, was a lean and shrivelled man.

CHAPTER XI.

REES PENNANT was physically brave, but the sight of those staring eyes meeting his in the bowels of the earth gave him a shock which, in the state of excitement into which his recent adventures had thrown him, for the moment caused his mind to lose its balance. He thought the man was alive, and, reeling, began to murmur some hoarse words of explanation of his own intrusion; but they came forth in indistinct, guttural sounds through the tube which covered his mouth. His hand shook so much that the dying light in his lantern went suddenly out, leaving him in utter darkness. Losing his head altogether, he uttered a wild cry, and would have burst himself loose both from tube and rope if a strong pull at the latter had not suddenly called him to remembrance of Sep faithfully waiting for him in the vaulted chamber above.

The fact was that Rees, in his efforts to get as far as the length of the tube would allow, had given the three pulls which he had arranged between them as the signal for Sep to help him to return. In spite of himself, therefore, he felt that he was drawn backwards. He had been pulled two or three steps when he heard the clink of his nailed boots against something on the floor, which, by the sound, he thought must be metal. Stopping, he groped on the ground, and had just time to pick up something small and round, which he fancied might be a coin, when a stronger pull then before at the rope round his waist dragged him away, and told him that Sep believed him to be in some dire emergency.

More and more rapidly he felt himself pulled along, until it was as much as he could do to save himself, in the darkness, from injury against the rough walls. When he reached the cliff, he was indeed thankful for the help the rope afforded him; for it rose almost sheer from the ground, with but few notches down the side on which the feet could rest. After that, however, the rest was comparatively easy. Impelled to increased speed by the fact that he was now nigh to suffocation, as poor Sep could not draw the rope and keep the tube straight at the same time, he reached the bottom of the upper staircase in very few moments, and tearing off the macintosh mask, drank in the air in great draughts.

"Are you all right, Rees? Are you all right?" asked Sep, in tones of deep anxiety.

"All right?" sang out the young fellow, in a voice which thrilled with triumph. "Yes, righter than I ever was in my life, for I've found Lord Hugh!"

Scrambling up the remaining steps, he flung himself down, panting, by the side of Sep, who threw his arms round him with genuine delight, which, to do him justice, was caused more by the sight of his companion safe and well than by the news he brought.

When Rees, now again feverish with excitement, told him his adventures in thrilling whispers, Sep was carried away with astonishment and delight, which reached their climax on the production of the piece of metal which Rees had picked up in the darkness. For this proved to be, as the latter had supposed, a coin, heavy, clumsy, of a fashion they had never seen; but it was gold, genuine gold. The young men looked at it, rubbed it, turned it over reverently in their hands. There was a romance about this gold, the property of a king long since passed out of reach of the need of it, and guarded for more than two centuries by a dead man, which appealed to the imagination.

"You think it was Lord Hugh of Thirsk I saw down there, don't you?" asked Rees in a low voice.

"Who else should it be? Did you notice his dress?"

"No, nothing but his eyes, staring straight at me, I tell you, like those of a living man. I thought he was alive. If he had been dead two hundred and forty years, he would be crumbled to dust, wouldn't he?"

"I don't know. Shall you go down there again?"

"No," answered Rees, with a shiver. "I don't think so. I—I suppose it's sentimentality, but even if he has down there with him the thousands that old beggar expects, I don't like the idea of robbing a dead man of what he's watched over for more than two hundred years."

"Well," said Sep, who, as usual, was ready to chime in with the views of his companion, "you mustn't let him know what you've found then; for he's a greedy old hunks, and as cynical as they make 'em. Let's keep him out of it altogether if we can."

The words were hardly out of his mouth when both were startled by Goodhare's voice. This gentleman, who was not likely to lose anything for want of a little watchfulness, had conceived the idea that something was likely to turn up this evening, and had managed, in his praiseworthy intention of looking after his own interests, to scale the outer wall of the castle with the help of the ivy. He heard Sep's words, but affected not to have done so, since any little resentment he might feel would "keep," and to show it now would be inconvenient and even dangerous.

"Are you there, boys?" he asked therefore in a low voice, speaking in a mild and patriarchal tone.

"Yes," answered Rees, with ill-humor which he did not hide.

He had slipped the old coin into his pocket at the first sound of the librarian's voice; but the action did not escape Goodhare's keen eyes. As the latter advanced and took his place slowly on the ground by the younger men, it was evident to him that something of great interest had occurred. The disordered and dirty state of Rees's clothes, the frayed rope, the excitement under which both young men were laboring, all spoke eloquently of some discovery.

"So you've been down, I see, and I see also that you've found something. Come, lad, out with it; I'm sure by your face that I did not set you to work in vain."

Rees moved uneasily.

"You seem to know more about it than I do myself," he said, rather sulkily. "I've risked my life over this business, and I've found a stopped-up passage certainly, but nothing of these thousands you talked about."

He could not, however, meet the eyes which were fixed steadily upon him.

"If you don't choose to tell me your adventures, Rees, at least you can trust me," the old man said at last with affecting simplicity. "So you won't be alarmed if I withdraw from a conference where I see I'm not wanted."

He was in the act of rising with much dignity when Rees drew him pettishly down again.

"Sit down; it's all right," said he. "Only you needn't bring more risk upon us by coming in to play the spy."

"Indeed, I think you might know me better than to suppose that was my intention. I——"

"All right," said Rees, cutting him short. "There, that's all I've found and the body of a dead man."

"A dead man!" cried Amos, who had clutched the old coin which Rees threw to him with greedy eagerness. "A dead man! Why, that must be Lord Hugh, and it's all true! This," he went on, turning over the gold piece in his lean fingers, "is a louis d'or. And there must be more—more!"

"That's all I found, at any rate," said Rees shortly.

"And you were content to come away with that, without hunting, searching, finding the great treasure which we may now be sure he had on him!" hissed out Goodhare, his mildness giving place to such burning fierceness of look and manner that it crossed the minds of both young men that he looked like a savage animal ready to spring upon Rees and tear his heart out.

"I was content to come away before I was suffocated, certainly," said Rees very quietly. "I would sooner die a few years later a beggar on the top of the earth than die now in the bowels of it with my hands full of gold. Besides, I didn't find any gold, except just that one piece. Probably they had drafts on bankers in those days just as they have now, and the fortune may turn out to be just a bit of faded and worthless paper."

This suggestion startled them all for a moment. Then, however, Goodhare shook his head.

"It is not probable," he said. "The money was brought from the one country to the other, and I should doubt whether the credit of the King of France was good enough in England for his draft for a large sum to be honored by any banker, even if the times had been more settled. No, depend upon it, if there was treasure sent it was in specie."

"Perhaps the chest he was sitting on—" began Rees.

"Chest!" echoed Goodhare impetuously; "there was a chest, you say! Surely you don't mean to let the night pass without ascertaining what is in it?"

"I do, though," said Rees frankly. "The journey down there and back, with the dangers of poisonous air on the one hand, and no air at all on the other, bruising one's limbs, and tearing one's flesh, is not to be undertaken every half hour."

Goodhare was white and very quiet, but they could see fiery anger and impatience in his eyes.

"Those who cannot face danger are not worthy of a great reward," he said sententiously.

"Face it yourself, then," answered young Pennant, and he brought the tube and the rope over to Goodhare. "We'll arrange all this for you, and as there are two of us, we shall be able to help you better than Sep could me."

Amos saw that the young man, fresh from his triumphant adventure, must be humored.

"Well, lads, you must forgive the impatience of an old man who has only a few years left in which to enjoy life," he said benignantly. "And now I think you both deserve a little merry-making for your pluck, so you must come home with me and share my humble supper."

He helped them actively in coiling up both rope and tube. The lantern Rees took home for examination, as the light it had given was by no means satisfactory. Then, for fear of possible watchers at the lodge, Goodhare and Sep were let down in the usual manner, while Rees walked out by the wicket-gate. Ten minutes later they were all at the librarian's lodging.

The younger men had expected nothing but the most frugal fare, and they were too much excited to have cared what was put before them. To their surprise, however, Goodhare had provided a game-pie, and on turning the key of a small corner cupboard which one would have supposed devoted to books, he revealed a small cellar of different wines of the choicest brands.

"Now, boys," said Goodhare in his most benevolent tones, "I shall not complain if you leave my cellar empty. For we shall soon be able to fill it again in London—glorious London. I had a presentiment that we should have something to celebrate to-night."

While he left the room for a corkscrew, Sep, to whom wine was an irresistible temptation, made a brief but close inspection of the bottles, at the end of which he turned to his friend with a dry laugh.

"The old fox made good use of his time up at the castle," he said.

Before the less suspicious Rees could make any inquiry, Amos had re-entered the room.

It was not difficult, in the state of high excitement into which his adventures had thrown him, to make Rees drink a great deal more wine than he had ever done in his life before, nor by artful suggestions, to tickle his imagination into the belief that a princely fortune lay at his feet ready to be enjoyed. At the same time, by rousing in Sep memories of his past dissipations, Amos managed to make him feel discontented with his present quiet life, and eager to indulge again in the old excesses. Thus the librarian secured a half unwilling ally in the corruption of Rees Pennant, who, from listening with disgust to their remarks on women, passed to laughter, and finally to a boastful share in the conversation. As for Lord St. Austell, when reference was made to him, Rees had no words strong enough to express his contempt and abhorrence for the man whose vices he had, a moment before, seemed anxious to emulate.

By midnight it was evident that, unless they wished to court a death-blow to all their plans by some indiscreet revelation on the part of Rees, his potations must cease. So Goodhare and Sep, better seasoned than he, escorted him home, and returned to continue their revels without him.

In this quiet country town, burglaries were so little feared that in many houses the front-door could be opened from the outside and was yet left unlocked at night. Rees, therefore, was able to let himself in without rousing the household. But when, as steadily as he could, he had stumbled upstairs and reached the landing, he met Deborah, in her dressing-gown, and with her hair arranged for the night in a long plait down her back.

"Oh, Rees, where have you been? I have been so frightened about you," she said in an anxious whisper.

For answer he flung his arm round her and gave her a kiss.

"Well, as long as you didn't tell, I'll forgive your fright, Deb, because it makes your eyes look so large and pretty," answered Rees, who had sense enough left to speak in a whisper.

The girl raised her little brass lamp and looked at him with a puzzled expression. There was a freedom in his manner, a boldness in his kiss, and something in his tone which made her blush crimson, and feel afraid of him. Having no idea of any of the causes of his excitement, she asked:

"Won't you come and say good-night to mamma? She's gone to bed, but she's been so anxious about you, for you never said you were going out."

Rees remained for a moment without answering. The mention of his mother brought a momentary feeling of shame to him. But then the evil effects of his recent experience again made themselves felt, poisoning Deborah's beauty to him. He pulled the girl down beside him on to the box-ottoman which stood in the corridor, and said vehemently:

"No, no; stay here and talk to me. Tell me it's true you love me, as they say you do."

Deborah, now beginning to suspect something, disengaged herself with the air of a Juno.

"I love you so much," she said with simple dignity, "that it gives me great pain to see you disgrace yourself. Go to your room now, as quickly and as quietly as you can."

Rees, overwhelmed with shame, and feeling for a moment as if the wind of an angel's wing had wafted away the mists of evil which had for months been creeping ever more closely round him, crept away, without so much as daring again to meet her eyes, to his own room.

CHAPTER XII.

NEXT morning Rees rose with a violent headache and a feeling that the whole world was out of joint. He was ashamed to meet Deborah, ashamed to meet his mother, and not in the mood to bear with Hervey's sententiousness. So he had a hurried breakfast alone, in a ground floor apartment, which was still, in memory of past glories, called the "housekeeper's room," and slipping out by the back garden door to avoid the rest of the household, he started for a walk by himself, full of remorse, full of great resolutions, and a determination that never again—no, never, for the sake of gold or for any other cause, would he consort with the satyr-like librarian, who seemed able, by a look, a word, to throw a taint upon all things fair and good.

Rees crossed the bridge, and sauntered along the banks of the river, instinctively choosing the direction which brought him face to face with the grey-walled ruins which had lately been the centre of all his dreams. At the first sight of the castle, in the hot morning sun, he felt that he hated it, connected as it was with all the disturbing forces which had been agitating his formerly happy life. But as he walked he began to feel that, whichever way he wished to look, those broken towers, those huge piles of rough stone, were the one point in the landscape to which his eyes must turn. They fascinated him: he watched the new and fantastic shapes which the jagged walls formed from every fresh bend in the river's banks with a sense that they now formed part of his life, and if that crumbling ruin were to disappear from the face of the earth the world would be empty for him.

He began to live over again, in spite of himself, the adventure of the night before; the descent of the two flights of steps, the cliff, the groping along the passage, the glassy stare of the dead man's eyes. Then suddenly he was struck with the idea that down under the ground, perhaps at that very moment underneath his feet, the dead messenger of a dead king was still keeping watch and ward over his master's gold. Out here in the staring sunshine, with the hot haze dancing over the narrow river, and the clang of the workmen's hammers coming to his ears from the shipbuilders' yards, all those experiences of the darkness seemed like a dream to him.

And yet he had seen it all with his own eyes, so he had to assure himself; and the old louis d'or which he had picked up among the dust of hundreds of years was still in his pocket. He drew it out and looked at it, and the coin seemed, by its incontrovertible reality, to put more practical thoughts into his head. That underground passage must have an end, an opening; and that opening would probably be on this side of the river. Slowly, thoughtfully, he retraced his steps, until he was exactly opposite the perpendicular cliff on which the castle, its foundations deep in the solid rock, stood.

The ground on which Rees was standing, on the opposite bank, was an open and very undulating meadow, under the numerous hillocks of which the imaginative could fancy the graves of the besieging Puritans to have been made. It was so open, indeed, so fully exposed, not only to passers by, but to occupants of the cattle lodge and of a couple of adjacent cottages, that Amos Goodhare, in his exhaustive scourings of the neighborhood, had never dared to carry on his researches there except at night.

Now Rees, less cautious, found himself strolling very slowly along with eyes fixed intently on the thick grass, which, cropped close by cattle on the higher ground, grew thick and lush at the water's edge. At last he sat down immediately opposite the window in the rock which gave light to the vaulted apartment in which his adventures had begun. His feet were only just above the sedge, and the grassy ground on which he was sitting was so soft from the heavy rains that he found a great slab of earth giving way under his weight, and sliding gently down with him towards the water. He scrambled up hastily, but in regaining his feet he caused the displaced earth to come down still faster, so that he fell down on his hands and knees and cut his left wrist against a stone. This stone proved to be the upper edge of a great slab of rock, which the freshly-moved turf had grown over and hidden. Rees drew a long breath. Was this the other entrance to the underground passage?

It was impossible to ascertain this now, in broad daylight, exposed to curious eyes. With a wildly beating heart, every thought but of the lost treasure again forgotten, Rees walked quickly away in the direction of the town library. He felt that he was bursting with this new discovery, that he must confide it to some one. Goodhare received him, seated in the library, surrounded by a pile of books of reference, the leaves of which he was busily turning for a pale, spectacled young man, who was taking notes by his side. Rees watched the librarian in amazement. It seemed scarcely conceivable that this grave, reverend-looking man, absorbed in intellectual work, and taking deep delight in it, could be the same creature whose eyes last night had shone with evil passions and almost ghoulish greed. In another moment, however, the spell was broken; Amos looked up, and there passed over his face the strange change which was like the peeping out of the spirit of evil through a hermit's eyes. He finished his work, however, after only a brief, respectful request to Rees to wait.

As soon as the spectacled young man had left them together, Rees, boiling with impatience, dashed across the room and communicated his discovery. Then they formed their plans for prosecuting the search, but, in their dread of prying eyes, decided to put off the execution of it until the next moonless night.

During the four following days, in the course of which they thought it prudent not to revisit the castle, all three of the conspirators lived in a state of intermittent fever, haunted by fears that some accident would lay bare to others the secret which the earth had so long hidden. These fears, however, proved unfounded. On the night when they all groped their way to the river bank with no other light than a dark lantern, they found the stone slab and the loosened earth exactly as Rees had left them.

Then began a task much heavier than they had expected. The stone was not far above high-water mark, and was situated near a bend in the river, so that the earth had accumulated upon it, especially at its base, during the ages which had elapsed since it was last displaced. The three men dug alternately for more than two hours and a half before there was any possibility of moving the stone. When they at last got clear of the surmounting obstructions, however, the task of raising the stone was comparatively an easy one. For, buried in the sand beside it, was a rusty iron bar, which they used, as it had evidently been used before, as a lever. The only thing which caused them still to doubt whether this was indeed the entrance to the passage was its extreme nearness to the water. However, all doubts on this point were soon set at rest; for, on raising the stone, they found that it covered the entrance to a narrow passage, not high enough even for a short man to stand upright in, which sloped rapidly down to the left, then, with a sharp curve, dipped more suddenly still to the right.

These facts Rees, who, armed with the miner's lantern, entered first, ascertained after a very few minutes' exploration. But at the bend the air grew so foul and heavy that he retreated, and again had recourse to his rope and his air tube. Thus equipped, he went on with his researches, and proceeding cautiously down the second incline, which was steep and exceedingly rough under the tread, he soon came to a third abrupt bend, after which the passage, now grown so much steeper that notches had been cut in the ground to help the passenger, turned again sharply in the opposite direction. When he had gone a few steps Rees stepped upon something, the sound of which set his heart beating violently and caused him to come to a dead stop. The incline was so abrupt that he had been walking with his head well back, feeling for each notch with careful feet. Stooping down he now saw that the ground was strewn with coins, grown dingy in the dust, but the reddish glitter of which, when he picked some up and rubbed them on his coat-sleeve, proclaimed them to be gold.

It was true then—the story of the lost treasure was true!

Rees climbed down the remaining steps, the nails in his boots clanking at almost every tread against more of the scattered coins. At last he was again on level ground. Stumbling against something, he heard the surging sound of a sea of gold pieces, and discovered at his feet a small clumsily fashioned chest, made of wood, covered with leather, and strengthened by metal bands. The lid was open, and the coins with which it had been filled were pouring from it. Rees scarcely noticed it.

For, not a yard from where he stood, was the dead Lord Hugh of Thirsk, the wide cavalier cloak still hanging in dusty folds from his fleshless shoulders, the low-crowned hat, with its ragged shred of feather, still lying at his feet.

Rees shuddered. This man, dying nobly in the execution of his desperate duty, reproached him—stung him with a half-acknowledged sense of a great difference. He stole closer, and by the lantern's weak light examined the motionless figure. The face was grey and shrivelled, the dry lips had fallen apart, and the glassy eyes stared out of cavernous sockets. Yet Rees fancied he saw the remains of a noble and handsome countenance in the wreck death had made. The hair fell, dark and lank and powdered with dust, upon the shoulders. The withered hands still rigidly clasped the thighs, as if their owner had determined with resolute strength of will to wait for death quietly. The low seat on which his body rested was formed of two small chests, of similar shape and size to that one against which Rees had stumbled.

Rough conjectures as to the events which had immediately preceded Lord Hugh's death flashed through Rees Pennant's mind as he made his way rapidly back to his companions, without disturbing by so much as a touch the solemn peace of the dead man.

No man, Rees supposed, could have carried more than one of those chests at a time. Small as they were, not more than twelve inches high, by ten wide, and eight deep, the weight of each when full of gold must have been great. Lord Hugh must have brought them down from the castle one by one when he resolved to try to escape by risking the unknown dangers of the disused subterranean passage. Rees pictured to himself that he must then have found his way to the other entrance, and either finding the stone impossible to raise, or discovering that he was in the midst of the Puritan camp, he had crept back, perhaps dashing to the ground in his despair the chest he had brought with him, and having failed in his enterprise, rather than fall either within or without the walls into the enemy's hands, he had sat down and calmly waited for death in the poisonous air.

This was the last of the romantic side of the adventure which Rees was allowed to see. With his return to Goodhare and Sep came the greedy, the base, the commonplace. When the opening of the entrance for some hours had allowed fresh air to mingle with the poisonous gases in the passage, which Rees's intrusion had moreover helped to disperse, in the cold grey light of the early morning Goodhare himself ventured to go down, followed by Sep, and, pushing aside the body with avaricious, ruthless hands, began to drag up one of the chests with long, lean, clutching fingers. Lord Hugh's dead body fell to the ground with very little noise, his long cloak in a moment losing its shroud-like dignity and splitting into ragged strips. Goodhare did not heed it; Sep glanced at it with a shudder; only Rees felt still the influence of the sentiment with which the sight of the poor cavalier had impressed him. Then back again they all went into the chilly morning air, carrying one of the chests with them. They worked all through the hours of early morning, until not a single coin was left in the cavernous passage of all the treasure which Lord Hugh had guarded so long. They did not attempt to carry it away then, as the daylight was growing strong, and at any moment they might be espied by some laborer on his way to work. Leaving the chests just within the entrance to the passage, they replaced the stone, and covered that over carefully with the clods of turf. Then, forced to trust to chance the safety of their fortune, they parted and returned as quickly as they could to their homes.

On the following night they removed the whole of the gold to Goodhare's lodging, where Amos made a rough calculation that the value of the gold, though much greater at the time it was first buried than now, would prove to be about fifteen thousand pounds. Rees made some faint suggestions about making known the discovery to Lord St. Austell; but Goodhare, while listening gravely, said it would be better for them first to take the gold up to London, and have the value decided by experts. To which Rees with little persuasion, and Sep without any, agreed.

They had made their plans for going to London, and Rees was, under the auspices of the two other men, looking forward to this new experience with vague delight, when Goodhare, who constantly affected to depreciate Deborah's charms, found an opportunity of meeting her alone as she was returning from some trifling errand for Mrs. Pennant.

Deborah had never tried to hide her dislike and fear of the librarian except by the barest show of civility, and therefore her surprise was unbounded when she suddenly found that he was making her an offer of marriage. When, not heeding her prompt refusal, he proceeded to tell her that he had just had a large sum of money left him, and could make her rich and independent, she drew herself up with much indignation.

"I don't think you understand women very well, Mr. Goodhare," she said coldly and proudly. "The first step towards marrying a man that I shall take will be to like him. That step, in your case, I have not taken."

Goodhare's face turned the ugly grey color to which any strong feeling brought it, and his eyes flashed.

"You are wasting your time waiting for Rees Pennant, Miss Audaer," he said, coolly; "he has other aims in view. In fact, perhaps I may say you have seen the last of him. If he does ever see you again, however, don't be surprised if he makes you proposals less honorable than those you have so very prettily rejected to-day."

Deborah broke away from him with an exclamation of disgust, and ran home as fast as she could, humiliated beyond expression by the man's offensive words and manner. She could not quite, try as hard as she might, dismiss some of his words about Rees as idle ones. The young fellow had gone out very early that morning, and had not yet returned, although it was past dinner-time. Tea-time passed, and still he did not come.

Then, overpowered by a dreadful presentiment, Deborah crept upstairs to the open door of his room, and finding it empty, went in. On the dressing-table was a note directed hastily in pencil to his mother. She carried it with a heavy heart to Mrs. Pennant.

It was as follows:—

"My dearest old mother,
"I am off; gone, not for long, but still gone. I have got a situation in London, and shall send you money every week, and come and see you very soon, be sure. I couldn't bear to say good-bye.—With all love, your ever affectionate son,

"REES."

Mrs. Pennant burst into tears.

"My brave, darling boy," she said, not willing to own she was hurt at this leave-taking, "he was quite right, as he always is. I could not have borne his going."

Deborah did not answer. A great fear blanched her cheeks. Goodhare had had money left him, and Rees had gone. After the words the librarian had used, she could not fail to connect the two facts. Was it in Goodhare's service that Rees was to be employed?

If so, the one being evil and the other weak, what power could save the man she loved from ruin?

CHAPTER XIII.

FOURTEEN months passed quickly and quietly away in the Pennant household, during which time the eldest son never once revisited his old home. At first Rees wrote to his mother regularly once a week. Very short indeed his notes were, but they were always warmly affectionate, and they always contained messages for Deborah and a remittance of thirty shillings or two pounds towards the house-keeping expenses. Poor Mrs. Pennant, who had been told how difficult to get situations in London were, was crazily proud of the immediate success of her favorite son, and only afraid that, in the wish to send her as much as he could, he was denying himself more than he ought to do.

Before long, however, these dutiful attentions began to fail. The remittances dropped off first, and the notes contained excuses, to which his doting mother replied by immediate assurances that she was in no need of money. This was now true. The energetic Godwin, who was acquitting himself admirably in his new position, sent home to his mother more than enough money to keep the little household in comfort. He also persuaded Hervey to apply for his own old situation in the Monmouth Bank, with many artful suggestions as to its being only for a time, and just to show people that a young man of unusual intellect could make himself a position anywhere. Hervey had swallowed the bait, got the situation, and, rather to his own disgust, proved a very good clerk. Once in the bank, therefore, he remained there, as Godwin had expected. For however high his soul might soar, and however far his great mind might roam, his great body had a habit of remaining docilely, in cabbage-like fashion, wherever circumstances placed it.

Both Hervey and Godwin remained as much in love with Deborah as ever, but she resisted steadily every attempt to break down the brotherly and sisterly relation between her and them. Godwin, in spite of discouragement, persisted, every time that he paid his mother a visit, in renewing his advances. But he did so in such a prosaic, matter-of-fact manner that Deborah could treat them as a joke.

"Are you still in the same mind, Deb?" he would ask in an off-hand tone, at the first opportunity when they were left together.

"About what?" she would say, affecting to have forgotten such a ridiculous trifle as his last proposal.

"About marrying me."

"Marrying you! Of course. What nonsense!"

"Very well, then, I hope you'll die an old maid," he would say viciously, to close the subject.

And Deborah would only laugh to herself in a contented manner, as if she felt that in that respect her fate was in her own hands.

As the girl was too handsome not to arouse envy among her own sex, she was often made to feel uncomfortably conscious that people believed she was pining for love of a man who did not care for her. Lord St. Austell, among others, tried to take advantage of this supposition. He had always been a great admirer of Deborah's rich and massive beauty, and as he belonged to that class of men who consider all women, in the position of dependents, fair game for their attentions, he now lost no opportunity of trying to ingratiate himself with her.

It was early in October of the year following Rees Pennant's departure from his home. Lord St. Austell, who was down for the cub-hunting, called upon Mrs. Pennant, and used all the genial charm of manner for which he was well known, in the endeavor to break down an instinctive shyness which the beautiful Miss Audaer had always left with him. But Deborah left him a good deal to Mrs. Pennant, who prided herself on being a brilliant talker and a woman of enduring fascination, and had had in her time ideas of becoming an Anglicised version of Madame Récamier. Not to be daunted, the earl called one morning before the old lady was prepared to receive visitors. She sent Deborah to the drawing-room with elaborate messages of regret, which Lord St. Austell quickly cut short.

"Well, Miss Audaer, it really doesn't matter, I only came to leave these papers for the old lady, and to ask" (and he dropped his voice confidentially), "whether you had any news of our old friend, Rees. I knew," he went on, "that if anybody had heard from him, it would be you."

Deborah blushed and looked very unhappy.

"No," she said. "For the last six weeks we have heard nothing. He hardly ever writes to me, only to mamma, and his notes are never very long. He travels about a great deal, he says, for the firm of lawyers he is with, and doesn't have much time for writing."

"Does he ever write to you, though, except from London?"

"No."

"Ah! And he is with a firm of lawyers, travels about, and was able from the first to send home two pounds a week?"

"Oh, he doesn't now. He hasn't sent any money for a long time."

"I wonder what the young beggar's up to?"

Lord St. Austell was walking up and down the room, and he said this half to himself. But Deborah, all passionate excitement, sprang up from her seat and placed herself right in front of him.

"What do you mean, Lord St. Austell?"

"Rees has been telling his mother a parcel of falsehoods, that's all. Do you think an idle, self-indulgent young scamp like that would get a salary large enough for him to spare two pounds a week? Do lawyers send their clerks scudding about all over the country like bagmen? No, Miss Audaer, our young friend is amusing himself, and doesn't want his mother to come up to interrupt his pleasures."

"But he has no money!" said Deborah, whose face expressed the strength of her feelings.

"How do you know? He manages to have the things that money gets, I happen to know, for not six weeks ago I saw him at Goodwood, perfectly dressed and perfectly mounted. Now, those are things which people can only do when they have either money or credit. The little beggar had the audacity to cut me, not that I bear him any malice for that," he added, good humoredly.

Poor Deborah was greatly troubled.

"He is so weak, so dreadfully weak; he must have got into bad hands," she said, in a quavering voice. "And yet, what can one do? Mamma will not go up to see him, because from the tone of his letters she can see he does not want her to. And she believes, or tries to believe, his constant promise of coming down to see us."

"Well, if you wait for that, you will have to wait until the young scapegrace has got to the end of his tether," said the earl, with a short laugh.

"But what am I to do? Mamma will believe nothing; indeed, I could scarcely wish her to. In the meantime——"

"In the meantime the lad may go one step too far, and the next news you have of him may be—through the newspapers."

Deborah drew her breath with a sob. These suggestions were only an echo to the fears which had lately been haunting her.

"I'll tell you what you could do," the earl went on, in a kindly, sympathetic voice. "You might discover an excuse for wanting to go to London; I am going up myself in a day or two, and you would be very welcome to my services as an escort, since I don't suppose they would let you travel alone. Then I would help you to find him out, and if he's got into some scrape, we'd do our best together to help him out again."

"Thank you," said Deborah, "I'll think about it."

The earl was delighted, thinking he had advanced a step. But the girl had the discretion which natural modesty imparts, and though she did give his proposition a second thought, it was with a slight alteration which he had not contemplated. The result of her reflections was that she put it into Mrs. Pennant's head that Rees might be ill, and that the best thing they could do was to go up and see him without too long a notice of their intention.

The discreet submissiveness towards the members of her family who were of the superior sex, which had become a habit of her life, made the old lady at first disinclined to act on Deborah's suggestion. But, by working upon her maternal fears, the girl at last induced Mrs. Pennant to write a note to Rees, at the address in St. Martin's-lane from which he always dated his letters, informing him that she was anxious about his health, and that she would call and see him within a few hours of the arrival of her note.

The two ladies left Carstow by the 4.12 train one raw October morning, before it was light. Hervey got up to see them off, but was just too late; they caught sight of him, panting and blinking on the platform, in the dull flicker of the gas-lamps, just as their train steamed out of the station. They had a dreadful, slow, stopping journey, and reached Paddington at ten minutes past ten, benumbed with cold, sleepy, and depressed. It was Deborah's first visit to London, and the sensations she experienced as they drove in a shaky four-wheeled cab across the town between Praed street and Trafalgar-square were mingled bewilderment and disappointment. For a film of brownish fog enveloped the houses and obscured the sun, gave a wet, greasy look to the pavements, and to the atmosphere a heaviness which seemed suffocating to the country girl.

"Oh, mamma, is this really London?" she asked, as, with her teeth chattering, she looked out of the window when they came to Oxford Circus.

"Yes, child; of course you know it is. This is where two of the principal streets cross each other," answered Mrs. Pennant, rather pettishly, for she was tired with the early and unaccustomed journey.

"What a pity we have come up on such a bad day! It makes everything look so black and gloomy."

"If we had come up any other day it would have been the same. London is always foggy at this time of year."

"Always like this?" cried Deborah, in amazement. "Why, how can people live in it?"

"They not only live in it, they like it."

"Well, then, now I can understand all one reads about the corrupting influences of a great city. For if people can grow to like this atmosphere better than the pure air, it is not astonishing that they can learn to like evil ways better than good ones."

Mrs. Pennant did not answer; she was too cross. They drove on in silence, Deborah filled with ever-increasing amazement and disgust. When at length the cab drew up at an old-fashioned and dingy house in St.

81

Martin's-lane, on the right hand side as you go down towards the church, she, however, could not suppress a low cry of horror.

"Oh, mamma," she cried, "surely poor Rees doesn't live here?"

"Don't be silly, Deborah, crying out like some gawky country cousin. Of course, London is not like Carstow."

They got out, and going up four much-worn stone steps, rang the bell, and were admitted by an old woman, who said that she didn't know whether Mr. Pennant had come home yet, but she would see. She turned and walked to the end of the hall, which was narrow, dingy, and dark. Knocking at a door on the right, she opened it without waiting for an answer and announced:

"Some ladies to see you, sir."

"Show them in," said a voice which neither recognised.

Mrs. Pennant and Deborah traversed the passage slowly, both prepared for some great change in Rees. Therefore, at the first moment of meeting, they were both inclined to think the alteration in him less great than it really was. The room was small and very dark, for the little daylight that filtered through the fog was obscured by the backs of the neighboring houses. The furniture was of the dingy kind peculiar to the back rooms of London lodging-houses, and the fire which burned in the small grate gave forth plenty of smoke, but little flame and less heat.

On a desk in front of the window were pens, ink, some sheets of blue foolscap, and a legal looking document, one pen lying as if it had recently been used. Rees was sitting by the fire, with a newspaper in his hand. He got up to meet them, but it was with more nervous excitement than pleasure that he kissed his mother and shook hands with Deborah. Both saw at once that he was much thinner than he used to be, and that the old boyish, light-hearted expression had left his face. But it was not until the flush which had come into his cheeks at their entrance had died away that they knew what a wreck of the Rees they had known and loved was before them. His cheeks were sallow and sunken, his eyes looked larger and blacker than ever, there were new lines and furrows forming about his mouth and eyes, and, greater change than all, the look which had been frank had become cynical and bold. Even these two simple ladies could see that many people—women especially—would have considered Rees handsomer now than in the old time, but yet both knew that the alteration in him was for the worse.

Mrs. Pennant affected to think that her son was overworked. Deborah, who assigned a very different cause to the change in him, wondered whether the reticent old lady was sincere. Rees explained that he had lost his situation at the lawyer's through no fault of his own, and that he was now keeping himself by law-copying at home. And he glanced at the desk.

Although he hurried this out in a mumbling tone, Mrs. Pennant made no indiscreet comments, but contented herself with caressing his curly head and murmuring, "Poor boy, poor boy!"

After an hour spent in the dingy little room, Rees asking many questions about the family and about Carstow, and leaving no opportunity for questions in return, Mrs. Pennant asked if he would come out and take them somewhere to lunch.

"You know," she explained gently, "we have had no breakfast."

"Indeed, mother, I wish I were in a place where I could have had a nice luncheon prepared for you. But I have only this little den and a couple of cupboards—for they're nothing more—on the second floor. And I'm too busy to go out. But I'll pack you up comfortably in a cab and send you to a place where I've been very well served in better times, and you might get your shopping done or whatever calls you may have to make; and by the time you come back here I'll have my work done. By-the-bye, Deborah," he went on, turning as if by an afterthought to the girl who had risen to go, "you might stay and help me to get this through, if you will. I can get on twice as fast if you'll dictate."

The girl hesitated, but Mrs. Pennant broke in at once:

"Yes, yes; stay, my dear, and help him to get his work done. I will be back in an hour—or two hours. Which shall it be, Rees?"

"I don't think we can get through in less than two hours, mother."

"Very well, then. In two hours I will be back."

The active old lady was already out of the room, Rees following, while Deborah, erect and very grave, waited for his return.

CHAPTER XIV.

WHEN Rees re-entered the room, he found Deborah standing at the desk examining the inkstand. It was quite dry.

"Ha! you've found me out," he said, laughing. "Of course, I didn't really want you to dictate for me. One doesn't waste the time of a lovely girl like that. Come and sit by the fire and talk to me. We have two hours before the old lady comes back."

He put his arm round her, drew her to the fire, made her sit in the arm-chair, from which he had risen, and placed himself on the hearth-rug at her feet.

"Now," he said, "we can talk."

"Yes," answered Deborah, who had been unusually grave and silent ever since her arrival.

"I say," he went on, looking up to examine her face with boldly critical eyes, "you've changed a good deal, Deborah, surely."

"Changed!" said she. "Have I 'gone of,' as they say?"

"No, it isn't that exactly; but you seem to have grown older, more staid, more demure. And—you dress differently, don't you?"

"I'm not wearing the same things that I wore a year ago, of course. I suppose you mean that I'm countrified beside the London ladies."

"You're much handsomer than they are, at any rate. I really think, Deborah, without any joking, that you are the handsomest woman I've ever seen."

"Well, you have something more interesting than that to tell me, I suppose. I want to know all about yourself; I'm not so submissive as mamma, remember, and you can't put me off as you can her."

"No, I'm afraid you're rather inclined to be strong-minded, Deb. No need to ask whether you're still heart whole and fancy free. No man would ever have the courage to make up to you."

"They have though; you will be surprised to hear that I've had two offers, and that I refused them both because I was *not* heart whole and fancy free."

Rees looked rather pleased. Grave, almost solemn as her manner was, there was a tell-tale shyness in her glance, a marked maidenly reserve about her actions, which told the already blasé young man that her interest in him was as strong as ever.

"I can guess who the offers were from," said he. "Godwin and Hervey."

"No," she said simply, "I didn't count them."

"Indeed, that's flattering to us poor Pennants, to hear we don't count."

Deborah said nothing to this.

"And in all this crowd of admirers, I suppose you never find time for a thought of me? Being a Pennant, I suppose I don't count either."

"I think of you a great deal," said Deborah quietly.

"And what is it you think of me? That you never want to see me again?" he asked, leaning coaxingly against her knee.

"I think," she said sorrowfully, "we never shall see the old Rees again."

"Did you care for the old Rees then?" asked the young man very softly, with a tender inflection in his voice which was altogether new to her, as he looked up into her face with pleading, passionate eyes.

The unsophisticated girl betrayed her secret altogether in a moment, as her body began to tremble, her cheeks to flush, and her eyes to fill. Rees at once seized his advantage. Crawling up to her side on his knees, he put his arm round her waist and leaned his head against her shoulder.

"Deb, Deb, you care for me still, don't you, whether I'm good or bad, whether I'm changed or not? If you knew that I wanted you, you'd come to me, wouldn't you, whatever they said? And you don't care for Godwin's frigid love-making, or for Hervey's virtuous homilies, but you love your poor Rees through everything, don't you, don't you, Deb?"

"Rees, you know that I love you," whispered the girl passionately.

"And if I asked you to come up and live near me, you would, wouldn't you, Deb? If you knew that I was ill, and wanted your care and your consolation? You wouldn't leave me to the care of that cock-eyed old lady who let you in, would you?"

"Oh, Rees, no! of course we wouldn't. But if you are ill, why don't you come home and be nursed? We live comfortably now. I'm housekeeper, and sometimes cook as well. And, oh! we should be so pleased and proud to take you home again!"

Rees listened to this speech rather impatiently.

"My dear child," he said, "I don't feel inclined at present to settle down to the old lady's tea and toast and prayer meetings. One may end in that, but it's a little too early as yet. The fact is," he went on hurriedly, as he saw her face change, "that I couldn't leave town just now, however much I wished it. A man has his living to get, a career to make, you know."

"And you want us to come up and live in London?"

"Well, I want you, Deborah—*you*—to get used to the thought of a London life. You see, my dearest child, I live a most harassing life, bound by ties and responsibilities that are a perpetual burden to me. I want some one near me who would be sweet and kind, and capable of self-sacrifice for a man she loved; who would bear with his caprices, keep him straight through his temptations, who would care nothing for the world, but only for him. It's a great deal to ask, Deborah; and I don't think there are many women capable of it."

The girl interrupted him by laughing softly. She was brimming over with happiness.

"Why, Rees, those things are not sacrifices to any woman worth her salt. Your London ladies must be poor creatures if they've taught you to think differently. And if I'm a little 'countrified' at first, as you seem to think, I promise you that in the pride of being your wife I shall soon grow into a very elegant person indeed."

"My wife!" said Rees, coming closer to her, and joining his arms round her waist. "Yes, that would be jolly, wouldn't it? For me to come home and find you waiting for me, making a lovely picture by the fireside. But you know, Deb, I'm very poor. I can't afford to marry yet. In the meantime I am slowly dying, I really believe, for want of the care that only a woman can give."

Deborah started and looked down with anxious solicitude into his face.

"Oh, Rees, you don't mean that. It can't be true! If it is, of course mamma and I must leave Carstow and come up at once to you."

"But you can't break up the old home like that," objected Rees, quickly. "It would be most unfair both to my mother and to Hervey."

"Yes, but if there is nothing else to be done to save your life, Rees, I know neither of them would hesitate for a moment."

Rees leapt up from the floor and began to pace up and down the little room in a state of high excitement.

At that moment there was heard the sound of a latch-key in the front door, and then steps along the passage. The door of the room was thrown open, and a well-dressed elderly man came quickly in. Deborah started up in astonishment.

"Lord St. Austell!" she exclaimed.

With a bow and a harsh laugh the man came nearer.

Rees stamped his foot, and said haughtily:

"Don't mention that wretch's name here."

Deborah looked at the new-comer again. It was Amos Goodhare. Except that he was evidently older, better-dressed, and that he lacked the earl's geniality of manner, Amos was the very counterpart of Lord St. Austell, down to the libertinism of expression which had always marred the earl's countenance.

The meeting gave the girl a great shock. Goodhare's presence poisoned all the pleasure she had felt in Rees's protestations of affection. With a sudden change to extreme dignity and reticence, she turned to Rees, and told him that she would go and find his mother; she was afraid something had happened to detain her. Then, before he could remember that she did not know where Mrs. Pennant was, Deborah shook hands with him, bowed coldly to Goodhare, and left the house.

Once outside in the street she did not know where to go. It was not much past midday, but already the fog was hanging in a thick brown veil over the houses; in a few hours even old Londoners would be unable to find their way from place to place. She turned to the left, and walking a few paces slowly up the street, found herself at the corner of a paved passage, which ran, between two rows of dismal, deserted houses, into Charing Cross-road. The entrance to this passage was flanked by high boardings, which were covered with flaming advertisement posters, among which there flaunted conspicuously the colossal portrait of a lady with a marvellous abundance of curly hair, whose eyes had been carefully picked out by the ubiquitous boy. Deborah gazed up at the houses with fascinated interest. They were old, almost ruinous. The windows, the glass of which had in nearly all cases disappeared, were covered by nailed-up boards. Most of these buildings had been small shops which had gone gradually down in the world, as was proved by the fact that in some cases two had been made out of what was originally one. The doors were nailed up as well as the windows, and pasted over the whole of the ground-floor walls were the dingy remains of more posters, which the damp had reduced to fluttering rags.

There was a look about these hole-and-corner beetle-browed little shops which would have suggested to a more sophisticated observer the unsavory literature of Holywell-street. To Deborah the place was eloquent only of black poverty and wretchedness, such as, in her pleasant country life, she had scarcely dreamed of. She glanced down the gratings into the disused cellars, full of dust and rubbish, then up at the great beam which had been put across from side to side at one end of the passage to keep the tottering buildings from falling in, while they awaited their impending demolition. As she raised her head and watched with a kind of horror the great clouds of mist and smoke that seemed to roll down towards the earth from the brown sky, she heard footsteps on the flags behind her, and turned with a start to see Amos Goodhare.

His mouth expanded with an ugly smile as his eyes met hers. The girl thought that he looked like the incarnate spirit of evil, and that his figure harmonised with the hideous surroundings.

"I am so pleased to see you, Miss Audaer," he said, courteously enough. His old pedagogic manners seemed to have given place to a burlesque of those of the earl. "But I am surprised, too, for I had heard that you were married."

"No," said Deborah, "I am not married."

"Well, I am jealously inclined to be glad that no unworthy wretch of a man has yet obtained a prize much too good for him. But matrimony seems to be in the air just now, and I didn't know whether you had yet fallen a victim. Rees and Lady Marion Cenarth are the last pair. But of course you've heard that. It's a secret at present, and I'm the letter-carrier."

He held out for her inspection a letter, stamped and directed to "M.C." at a shop in South Audley-street.

Deborah was for the moment so absolutely stunned as to be incapable, not only of showing, but of feeling anything. She looked at the envelope and appeared to be examining the address, which she perceived to be in Rees's handwriting. She was intelligent enough to understand in a moment the meaning of Rees's strange love-making and the extent to which the evil influence of the man before her had corrupted the unhappy lad. At the same time there sprang up in her mind a defiant determination that this depraved Goodhare should not triumph in her humiliation.

"I did not know of it," she said at last, very quietly, "though I rather guessed at something of the sort from his manner. Are they already married then?" she went on; and, having quite recovered her serenity she looked up in his face.

Goodhare was puzzled, disappointed. This she saw and hated him for.

"I'm not sure whether they're married yet," he said; "but, at any rate, they're going to be. They've been corresponding all this year."

"Oh dear, I hope the earl won't be very angry."

Goodhare's face, as usual, grew black at the mention of the earl's name.

"I don't know, I'm sure," he said, shortly. "But I don't suppose he'll be pleased."

"I do hope, though, that he'll forgive them very soon. But now I must say good-bye to you, Mr. Goodhare, for my mother must be by this time waiting for me at Rees's lodgings."

She bowed to him, and turning, walked rapidly back to St. Martin's-lane, where she found Mrs. Pennant in the act of getting out a cab.

"What is the matter, my dear? You look so dreadfully white," cried the old lady on seeing her.

The girl ran up and clung to her hand.

"Mamma, mamma, don't go in again, or if you do, let me go away without you," she whispered in a hoarse voice. "I cannot bear it."

Mrs. Pennant was a strangely reticent woman, whose thoughts were difficult to guess. She turned as pale as the girl herself, however, and drawing her into the cab without more inquiries, directed the cabman to drive to Paddington.

The two ladies reached Carstow late that night; but neither during the journey, on their arrival, nor ever afterwards, did they exchange confidences on the subject of the impressions the visit to Rees had left on their minds.

In the meantime the first thick fog of the season was settling down steadily over London, and when Amos Goodhare rejoined Rees in the little back room, the gas which they were obliged to light shone dimly through a murky mist. The young man lay stretched on the narrow sofa.

"Where is she?" he cried, starting up, with dishevelled hair and wild eyes.

"Who? Lady Marion?" asked Goodhare lightly.

"Lady Marion! No, d—— Lady Marion. I mean Deborah—my beautiful Deborah! I will see her—I must! If she will have me, I'll give up all thoughts of that lanky caricature of a woman, beg her to forgive me, and marry her."

"Too late, too late, my impulsive young friend. 'Your' beautiful Deborah is on her way back to Carstow, too utterly disgusted with you to give you another thought."

"But, Goodhare, she did not understand. She is too pure, too good to believe that men can be such blackguards as you have made me. Let me go, I tell you, let me go!"

He struggled to pass Goodhare, who locked the door and put the key in his pocket.

"I am not going to have that poor girl insulted any more," he said. "If she did not understand what you meant while she was with you, she did before she left London."

"You infernal scoundrel! You told her! You explained to her! You have ruined and degraded me, and you wanted to make me ruin and degrade her!"

He flew at the elder man, who held him off with long, sinewy hands, as he could not have done before the once athletic young man had become weakened by excesses and dissipation.

"*You* degrade her! *You* degrade that girl!" said Amos, letting the contempt he felt for his poor tool shine for once full from his eyes; "women of her sort are not degraded by such as you, nor by such as I either. You have to marry Lady Marion. I had to bring that about by any means I could. That's explanation enough. And now to business."

He let the young man go, for Rees Pennant's outburst of anger had already given place to sullen passivity, and he had thrown himself limply into a chair. Goodhare took a seat beside him.

"Listen," he said, "I have something to say to you. You know that we have come to the end of our money?" Rees nodded. "And of our credit?" Rees nodded again. "That at present there are no more new clothes to wear, horses to ride, evenings at the theater, suppers afterwards, trips to Paris, and the rest of it?"

"Well, of course, I know it. Hasn't every caller been a dun, and every letter a bill, for weeks past?"

"Quite so. Now the question is, whether you want any more of those past pleasures, or whether you would prefer to set to work as a clerk on twenty shillings a week, or to creep back to Carstow, and live on the charity of your younger brothers?"

Rees writhed.

"Out with it. What do you want me to do? You know you have made work impossible to me; quiet life in the country insupportable. What have I got to do?"

"Well, I suppose you know that, in the straits we are in, one mustn't be too particular."

"I can't be a lower rascal than I showed myself this morning. Go on."

"Put on your hat, button up your overcoat, and come out."

"Out! What, in this fog, that's almost blinding even indoors?"

"Yes. I found you one fortune in the bowels of the earth. The second we must hunt for in the dim recesses of the air."

With a short laugh Goodhare rose, and waited while Rees slowly prepared himself for the walk.

When they reached the street the brown mist was already so thick that the houses on the opposite side of the way were scarcely visible. Goodhare drew his young companion's arm through his with a laugh.

"Look at this beautiful atmosphere," he said; "feel it, hug it up to you. Talk of the blue skies of Italy! I wouldn't give twopence for the brightest of them. These sweet, fair brown skies were made for rogues—like you and me."

Rees shuddered, but he did not dispute the point.

Slowly, through the ever-thickening fog-cloud, they made their way together towards Trafalgar-square.

CHAPTER XV.

FOR months Deborah Audaer suffered from the horrible effect which the incidents of the visit to Rees had left upon her mind. London seemed to her the pestilential centre of all evil, physical and moral. The inky atmosphere, the black, gloomy streets, Rees Pennant's dingy room, the passage full of deserted, dirty houses, all contributed to form a ghastly background to the picture of evil in which Amos Goodhare, with his cynical stare, and Rees, with his bold, feverish eyes, formed the central figures.

That journey had shown her men and things from a new and hideous point of view. For a time all the sweetness and freshness of life seemed poisoned for her. She saw the ills in the world—poverty, sin, and sorrow, in a harder, colder light. Since Rees whom she loved, could be corrupt and base, what in the wide world could be pure? So she reasoned, womanlike, and suffered in silence for the rest of the year, seeing a new and uglier sadness in the autumn and winter changes of nature, and brooding over her poor lost ideal.

Deborah was much too brave and good a girl for this change in her thoughts and feelings to find outward expression in her actions. Whatever view she might take of life in the abstract, the round of daily duties, which were sufficiently heavy, were fulfilled just as well as ever, and if Mrs. Pennant was shrewd enough to detect a change in the girl, it was not by finding the thin places in the old drawing-room curtains less carefully darned or her early cup of tea forgotten. For Deborah, to save the expense of keeping more than one servant, was perfect mistress of every household duty. This extreme domestic devotion, as Godwin considered it, excited in him great annoyance, the more so that he was now enjoying a salary which enabled him to send home a very handsome allowance.

Soon after the eventful visit to London, Godwin paid his mother a Saturday to Monday visit, and took the opportunity of the old lady's afternoon nap to make a formal remonstrance with Deborah.

She was sitting on the old-fashioned fender-stool by the drawing-room fire, stroking the head of his fox terrier, when he came very softly down the long, cold-looking room, and stood behind her. She was bending down over the dog, talking to him softly; but presently, lifting up her head and perceiving the blocking out of the light from the window behind her, she turned with a start.

"Oh, Godwin, you startled me! I didn't hear you come in. I thought you'd gone over to Llancader."

"I changed my mind; I wanted to have a talk with you." Deborah moved impatiently. He went on quickly, noticing this movement, "Oh, not on the old subject; don't be afraid. I see you are not in the mood for one of my matter-of-fact proposals. I'm not even going to ask you why you are so particularly brusque, not to say snappish, to me this time. But I want to know why you don't keep another servant. You know very well that, with what I send to her, my mother can afford it."

Deborah, who had got up from the fender-stool and seated herself firmly on a chair, spoke very coldly and decisively.

"Is there anything wrong about the house, then—dirty windows, unswept carpets, or bad cooking—that you are dissatisfied with our arrangement?"

Godwin bounced up from the chair he had taken, and, standing with his back to the fireplace, stared over her head defiantly.

"Well, of all the disagreeable, bad-tempered girls I ever met, you are the most impossible to do anything with," he said, at last losing his temper. "What do you suppose I want you to keep another servant for, except to save you trouble? Considering that I don't live at home, what would it matter to me if the washing were hung over the front garden wall, and the knives cleaned on the drawing-room table?"

"What are you grumbling for, then?"

"I was not grumbling at all. I merely thought that a second servant would allow you to have more time to yourself."

"That was not your reason at all. You thought it more in accordance with the family dignity—that is, your dignity—that there should be two servants in your mother's house."

Godwin brought his eyes quickly down from the window, and looked at her with a keenness which made her uncomfortable.

"You are unhappy," he said at last, shortly, and not at all tenderly. "You never used to fish among people's motives for a mean one like that. You have had some annoyance or disappointment, and, like an unreasoning woman, you visit it on me, because you think you can hurt me. But you shan't! you shan't!"

And he put his hands in his pockets, and walked away up the room with a defiant air.

Deborah felt sorry and ashamed. He was quite right, and she knew it.

All women, when they have had their belief in man in the abstract destroyed by the perfidy of one particular individual, like to visit their disappointment and resentment upon some other individual whom they at the bottom of their hearts know that they can implicitly trust. If he had known it, therefore, Deborah's snappishness, which she reserved for him alone, was only the natural expression of her indignation that he, the man she did not love, was sound to the core, while the man she did love had proved himself a contemptible wretch.

She was not going to own herself in the wrong, though. Oh, no! She bit her lips with a moment's self-reproach, and then said, quite coldly:

"Whether I am happy or not is, you will admit, my own affair. Whether we keep one servant or twenty is, I admit, yours, since you pay them. But I tell you frankly that I feel much more comfortable with only one, because like that, by careful management and without any pinching, I am saving a large sum out of the money you send mamma, which she means to give you to furnish your house when you marry."

Of course Deborah knew that she was hurting him, though she would not have owned it.

"How dare you talk of my marrying?" he burst out, almost dancing . with rage. "You know I don't mean to marry; you know you don't want me to marry."

He had gone a little too near the truth. Naturally enough, Deborah would not have liked to see her own devoted admirer enslaved by another woman, however indifferent to him she herself might be. She gave him one look of speechless indignation, and without heeding the grovelling apologies which he hurriedly began to make, sailed out of the room with the dignity of an empress.

She would not speak to him for the remainder of his short visit, except such few words as were absolutely necessary; and these she uttered in a loftily distant tone. Poor Mrs. Pennant saw that something was wrong, and make several discreet, but ineffectual, efforts to put it right. Deborah even took care to be out of the way when, on the following morning, Godwin went away again.

Mrs. Pennant heard very little from her other absent son, her darling Rees, although she wrote to him regularly. Indeed, as winter drew on, her letters became more frequent than ever, for the London papers published alarming accounts of a gang of skilful and desperate thieves, who, taking advantage of the foggy season, which was now at its height, waylaid well-dressed men even in much-frequented thoroughfares, and robbed them of everything of value they had about them, often with considerable violence. Rees's answers to his mother's letters were always very short; but he re-assured her as to his personal safety and also as to his prospects. He had got another situation, he said, better than the last, and was saving money. However, he sent home no proof of his altered fortune until Christmas, when Mrs. Pennant received from him a parcel containing a handsome fur collar and muff for herself and a beautiful chased silver clasp for Deborah.

The girl took her gifts in silence, and interrupted by no comment Mrs. Pennant's ecstasies. It was Christmas Eve, and Godwin, who was expected home, had already sent his presents.

"Why, Deborah, Deborah, this clasp is the very thing for the mantle Godwin has given you!"

"Yes, mamma," answered the girl, quietly.

But on the following morning, when she put on her new cloak to go to church with Mrs. Pennant and her sons, the clasp was not on it. The old lady remarked on this with some displeasure, thinking her eldest son's gift despised. Deborah, however, steadily excused herself from wearing it, and there was a slight coolness in consequence between the ladies, which resulted in Mrs. Pennant walking with Hervey instead of with her adopted daughter, and leaving the latter to follow with Godwin.

"Why won't you wear Rees's present, Deb?" ventured Godwin, diffidently, as they walked along. "No such luck as that you have give up thinking about him, I suppose?"

"No," answered the girl in a tremulous voice; "but don't let us talk about Rees; I can't tell you why, but I can't bear it."

He walked on by her side, obediently changing the subject. Only just before they passed under the heavy porch of the old Norman church, he asked:

"May I walk home too with you, Deb? I won't talk about anything to—to worry you."

"Of course," answered she, with a gentle and grateful smile.

But when the service was over and the congregation poured out of the church, Deborah was seized and surrounded by the Llancader ladies, who had come to Monmouthshire to pass Christmas. Only Lady Marion was absent. Deborah inquired after her of Lady Kate.

"Oh, don't you know. Of course, it's a secret, but still it's one that everyone seems to know—except papa and mamma," babbled out Lady Kate, in a confidential tone. "Marion is so dreadfully, idiotically fond of that Rees of yours that she has gone to stay with Aunt Lucilla, in Eaton Square, so that she may stay in the same town with him. She is making a perfect fool of herself about him. I must say so, Mr. Pennant, though I know he is your brother."

"Oh, I'm not at all offended, Lady Kate. You can't expect two geniuses in one family. But I think its a pity Lord St. Austell isn't told of their pranks."

"Nobody dares tell papa anything since last Friday," answered Kate in a lower voice.

"He was knocked down and robbed as he was walking at night with one of his friends. He had been out to dinner, and it was so foggy that he dared not drive home. And—of course we are not supposed to talk about it—but he believes he recognised one of the men who attacked him."

"Who was it?" asked Godwin, interested.

"Why—you won't say anything about it, will you?—but he thinks the man who knocked him down was the man who used to be librarian here—Amos Goodhare!"

"By Jove!" cried Godwin. "You don't mean it?"

"Yes, I do. This man struck papa down quite savagely, and held him down, and was going to kick him as he lay on the ground if one of the men with him—there were three altogether—had not interfered."

A sharply uttered exclamation burst from Deborah's lips. Godwin and Lady Kate turned quickly, and saw that the color had left her cheeks and that her face wore a terror-struck expression.

"What is the matter, dear?" asked plump little Lady Kate, in much concern.

"Nothing, nothing. I—I was only thinking—of—of what a narrow escape your father might have had with those—ruffians, and how glad I am that one of them had the humanity to save him from being hurt."

"Yes, indeed, we were surprised ourselves at that. It is quite like Claude Duval and the days of chivalry, isn't it? But I mustn't laugh about it for really poor papa has a dreadful bruise at the back of his head, and he might have been killed, of course."

"Yes, I—I am very thankful," said Deborah.

Godwin saw that something was the matter, and he managed to cut short Lady Kate's chatter, so that he could take Deborah home. But not all his artfully made suggestions and inquiries could drag from her the secret of the fear which made her creep about with startled eyes and a terror-struck white face all through that Christmas Day.

CHAPTER XVI.

REES meanwhile was spending his Christmas at his lodgings in St. Martin's-lane, with the faithful Sep Jocelyn for company. Sep was still as much outwardly devoted as ever to his more brilliant friend; but the fast life they were leading, acting upon a constitution already weakened by former excesses, was telling upon him even more plainly than upon the younger man. Sep was losing his nerve. As he sat with Rees by the fire on the evening of Christmas Day, heavy with late sleep and with a drinking bout of the previous night, every slight noise made by a movement of his companion, or by the traffic in the street outside, caused him to start, and sometimes to shiver. He had grown much older looking during the past year; his face was swollen and puckered about the eyes, while the threads of grey in his fair hair had multiplied into wide white streaks. His starts and tremors began to irritate Rees, who put out his hand to stop Sep as the latter was about to help himself from a decanter which stood on the table.

"That will do, Sep. Goodhare will be here in a minute to settle our next plans, and you'll want all your wits about you."

"But I'm so cold," pleaded the other, in a husky voice.

"Well, brandy won't warm you. Sit nearer to the fire."

"I can't get any nearer, unless I sit in the fender," complained Sep, rather sullenly.

For Rees had used rather a bullying tone.

"I'm going into a decline, I think," Sep began again. "This life's too much for me, what with the danger, and the work, and the risks, and then the pace we go when we're in funds."

"Do you want to go back to Carstow and your old auntie, then?" asked Rees, with what was meant for a sneer, but which proved to be a rather feeble one.

"No-o; at least if I did, I suppose you wouldn't let me go; and if you would, Goodhare wouldn't," said Sep, hopelessly.

The idea of starting an independent course of action was now further than ever beyond his capacity.

"I shouldn't prevent you," said Rees, gloomily. "This occupation of gentlemanly footpad is not more to my taste than to yours. I believe Goodhare likes violence; it's one vent to the savagery he has been saving up all these years. But, for my part, if I had my chances over again, I should choose life in the country with——"

He stopped.

"With Deborah Audaer?" suggested Sep.

Rees got up and stretched himself.

"What's the use of talking, when there's one of Marion's ecstatic effusions to be answered, and Goodhare may be in any minute."

"I'm sick of Goodhare, Rees; aren't you? He's a selfish, greedy old rascal, and he always contrives to get the lion's share of the plunder and the fox's share of the risk. He hardly lets one call one's soul one's own."

"Have we any souls?" said Rees. "I don't feel as if I had any such relic of respectability about me. Whatever I may have had left of that sort Deborah took away with her the day she came here with my mother. When I'm tired of this life I shall go to Carstow and claim it back from her."

"Do you think, Rees," suggested Sep, after a pause, "that a man who's led the sort of life we have is—is—well—quite good enough for a woman like Miss Audaer?"

"My dear boy, why trouble ourselves with questions of that sort? As long as they'll have us and worship us, no matter what sort of lives we've led, why should we worry ourselves by trying to lead any better?"

"And you think Miss Audaer worships you still?"

Rees got up, swaggered confidently across the room to his desk, unlocked it, and took from an inner drawer a woman's little morocco purse, which he flung across the table carelessly to his companion.

"Look inside," said he.

Sep opened it almost reverently, and found that it contained ten sovereigns.

"Her savings for half a year at least," explained Rees. "The day she came here she left it on the desk, sliding it under a piece of blotting paper, because she knew I was badly off. You see I have not touched it," he added, magnanimously.

"So I should think," said Sep, laconically. "Are you sure, though, Rees, whether she left it at the beginning or the end of her visit—on her coming in or on her going away?"

"What do you mean?" asked Rees sharply.

"Why, that perhaps she left it for the old Rees, whom she had known, and would not have left it for the new Rees whom she had to learn to know."

Limp and undecided in action, Sep was shrewd of thought and could be plain of speech. Rees received his suggestion very haughtily, and the two men were on the verge of a quarrel when the sound of the turn of a latch-key in the front door caused them instantly to drop their voices. For mistrust of their elder was the bond on which the friendship between the two younger men now chiefly rested.

Amos Goodhare entered in brisk and jaunty fashion. He alone of the three seemed to have found their alternately riotous and risky life perfectly agreeable to his tastes and constitution. After having grown old in the pursuit of learning, he was now growing young again at the fountain of pleasure. If he had lost something in dignity, he had gained in distinction, and the man on whom all had looked as an intellectual marvel seemed now remarkable rather for his well-cut clothes and the easy condescension of his manner.

"Well, boys," was his greeting, "you don't seem to understand how to make Christmas merry. I've come to show you how it can be made useful."

"By taking a lesson at Drury Lane, perhaps, and buttering the pavement outside rich old gentlemen's doors," suggested Rees ironically.

Amos gave the young man a glance of no particular warmth and said:

"No, not exactly that. We have a game in hand that nobody, I think, need despise for its facility. What do you say, boys, to carrying off the Crown jewels, or at least part of them?"

"I should say it was a very bad joke, and might, if indulged in, lead to a very good term of penal servitude," answered Rees, picking out a cigar very carefully from the case Goodhare offered.

"But I suppose that, like many other bad jokes, you won't be unwilling to lend a hand to carry it out."

Rees considered a few moments, and then laughed.

"No," said he. "It would be a new sensation, at all events."

But Sep began to shiver, and to look with glances of alarm from the one to the other.

"Leave me out this time, Goodhare," he said at last, hoarsely.

"Can't, my dear boy. Your shrewdness and methodical way of carrying out instructions is just as necessary to our combination as Rees's dash and my inventiveness. You sketch, don't you?"

"Ye-es, a little," admitted Sep reluctantly.

"And you have been in America, and could get up, I suppose, very fairly as artist and correspondent to a New York paper?"

"If I must, I suppose I could."

"And you, Rees," continued Amos, "who can do anything which needs smartness and dexterity of fingers, can use a file, or could learn to do it?"

"I could learn to do it, of course."

"Very well, then. The Christmas holidays are now on, and people flock to the Tower in swarms. By-the-by, I suppose that you know that St. Austell's brother, the Honorable Charles Cenarth, is keeper of the regalia?"

Rees started.

"Why on earth can't you leave that family alone, Goodhare?"

Amos laughed harshly, and a look of diabolical malice flashed out of his eyes.

"Oh, in this case my reason will explain itself as it goes on," said he. "In the meantime you will both, in the course of the holidays, visit the Tower more than once to familiarise yourselves with it. Go on Mondays and Saturdays, the free days, when there is a crush. Use disguise, but of the simplest and neatest sort. Rees, you will practise the filing away of iron bars without noise. And there is something else for you to do. Lord Wenlock, the general, is a great chum of St. Austell's, isn't he?"

"I believe so."

"Have you ever seen any of his handwriting?"

"Not that I remember."

"Then you must get Lady Marion to procure you a couple of his letters. Say they're for autographs. Study the handwriting, and then forge a letter requesting the keeper to give the bearer (whom you will call an American journalist of note), permission to sketch the regalia. I think you will find these instructions enough for the present."

"Yes, quite enough to land us at Portland," said Rees, cheerfully.

Reckless as impunity in crime had made him, he was not dull enough to ignore the stupendous risk of such a colossal piece of knavery. But the excitement of carrying out Goodhare's daring plans had now become necessary to his jaded senses, on which the risks of smaller and meaner thefts were beginning to pall. Trusting, therefore, to the fertile invention of the elder man for the details of the plot, he at once set to work on the preliminaries Amos had suggested, and persuaded the reluctant Sep to do the same.

Weeks passed on, during which Amos put the younger men through their paces with regard to their recently acquired knowledge of the geography of the Tower, tested Rees's progress in the art of using a file expeditiously and without noise, and caused him to forge letters from Lord Wenlock, until he produced one which the general himself might have mistaken for the production of his own pen.

Then, when all was ready, came a spell of bright weather; and Amos, who had implicit faith in the disorganising powers of fog, waited until the kindly brown cloak was again drawn over the sky.

One morning in the middle of February he announced that all was ready, and that the attempt would be made that day. Sep, whom Amos had kept under his own eye for a week or more, made his way through a thick sepia-colored mist to the Tower, presented the forged letter, and after only a short delay was admitted to the Wakefield, or Record, Tower, where the Crown jewels were kept, and accommodated with a seat.

The day was so dark, and the consequent difficulties of locomotion were so great, that only very few visitors came to the tower at all. These few were chiefly of the country cousin sort, and those who came into the Record Tower did not scruple to crowd round Sep, and to pass their opinion, in loud whispers, on the merits of the series of neat little pen-and-ink drawings which he was making from different points of view, so that from time to time the warder, who stood at the door, had to come forward and beg them not to interrupt the gentleman.

Presently, in the midst of a small batch of strangely-dressed people fresh from the colonies, there sauntered in, guide-book in hand, a young fellow of rather rustic appearance, dressed in the sort of clothes a respectable carpenter might wear for his Sunday suit. He was greatly interested in the work of the artist, who was making his way, by easy stages, all round the great cage, in the centre of the small stone room, in which the Crown and other jewels are kept. Wherever the American artist stopped, the young carpenter stopped too, carried away by his interest in the sketches. The warder, who never remained for many minutes out of the room, grew interested also, and watched the progress of the little pictures with much admiration. The day was so dark, and the fog so thick even inside the stone chamber, that the gas jets between the deeply-embrasured windows were all alight, giving to the precious gems a fiery lustre as they glittered through the murky atmosphere.

Sep had almost reached that side of the room which was furthest from the door when a tall, well-dressed man appeared at the entrance, and peeping in, said in cheery tones:

"Hallo! you've got an illumination up here, I see! What a mistake it is, this showing the State jewels at sixpence a head, like the Chamber of Horrors at a waxworks! What do you think, warder?"

"Well, I don't know, my lord; they're the people's treasures after all, and it pleases them to see 'em."

At the words "my lord," the American correspondent and the young carpenter looked around. The latter started. Seen by a cursory observer, not careful to mark trifling differences of stature and feature, the easy-mannered gentleman at the door, who wore an overcoat of "horsey" cut, and carried a small dressing-bag, would have passed for Lord St. Austell.

"I find my brother is not in," went on Amos, still in the earl's well-known genial manner, "so I've come up for a chat with you. They wanted to stop my bag at the gate—for a dynamitard's, I suppose. But the sight of my hair brushes and pomatum pots reassured them, I believe. You can keep it under your own eye, at any rate."

And the pseudo earl threw his bag down inside the doorway of the stone chamber, and proceeded to ask the alarmed warder if he had heard that it was proposed to do away with the body of men of which he formed so distinguished and ornamental a member, and to replace them with a staff chosen from the ranks of the metropolitan police.

The alarmed warder listened in consternation to this suggestion, which, coming from the lips of a gentleman who had so much access to persons in authority as the Earl of St. Austell, bore a frightful impress of probability. They discussed the rumor with much warmth, the sham nobleman growing even more excited and loud than the warder. A few visitors passed into the chamber and out again, while still the noble visitor and the alarmed guardian conversed at the door. With the last batch came the young carpenter and the American, the latter full of thanks to the warder for his courteous assistance. Still they discussed, the poor veteran much comforted, in the midst of his alarm, by the promise of his noble companion to "use his influence" for him and the body to which he belonged.

At last, however, with a start, the gentleman affected to remember that his brother, the Honorable Charles Cenarth, would have returned and be waiting for him. Snatching up his bag, he thrust a half-sovereign into the warder's hand, and made his way in a sauntering, jaunty manner, down the stone staircase.

That handsome "tip" was, however, dearly bought. A quarter of an hour later the poor warder, having recovered his equanimity a little, made his accustomed perfunctory tour of the chamber in which the Crown jewels lay. At the innermost point of the stone apartment he stopped, sick with horror. Some of the jewels were gone.

With clammy, trembling hands, the unhappy man touched the cage, behind the bars of which the treasures had seemed so safe. They gave way at the touch. The bars had been filed through, the glass neatly and noiselessly cut, and the jewels taken without the least warning sound. In a moment the whole building rang with the alarm. The soldiers turned out, the gates were closed, the few visitors still groping their way about in the fog were closely searched—all to no purpose.

By that time there was a bundle of clothes—"horsey" overcoat, carpenter's suit, American tourist's rig out—sinking, heavily-weighted, to the bottom of the Thames; while Amos Goodhare, Sep, and Rees were finding their way to the lodging in St. Martin's-lane by different routes.

An hour later there lay on the table in the dingy back sitting-room two Royal crowns—the so-called Queen's diadem, a massive circlet set with pearls and diamonds of enormous size, and St. Edward's golden crown, a larger and still more magnificent treasure, ablaze with precious stones. Besides these lay an old golden spoon and a collar studded with gems.

The three plotters, having carried through their adventures so successfully, stood staring at their treasure in bewilderment.

For even Amos, the oldest and craftiest, began to understand, in the face of this splendid prize, that they were very much in the position of gentlemen who, having obscurity as their only hope of safety, find themselves suddenly the possessors of a fine white elephant.

CHAPTER XVII.

AMOS GOODHARE was the first to recover from the sort of stupefaction into which the sight of their royal plunder had thrown the three confederates.

"Well, boys," he said, "I think we may rest on our laurels a little while after this feat. It would take an expert in jewels, which I don't profess to be, to tell you what value we have there. But here is a diamond in this," and he took up the diadem, "which cannot, I should think, be worth less than five thousand pounds. While this crown," and he laid his hand upon the other and still more magnificent prize, "ought to bring us in enough to live in modest comfort for the remainder of our lives."

"Well, there can't be much of them left to run at the rate we're going on," moaned Sep, who was altogether unhinged by the life of enforced abstinence he had led for the last few days under Goodhare's supervision, by the risks of the morning, and by the still greater risks in the disposal of the jewels which he knew would fall to his share.

"Sep, you're out of sorts. Drink a health to the Honorable Charles Cenarth, keeper of the regalia, and may he come half as easily out of this scrape as we have done!"

He went to the little rickety sideboard, and, taking out a decanter and glasses, filled three bumpers, and pushed one over to Sep, who emptied part of the spirit into another tumbler, and drank the rest, diluted with two-thirds of water.

"Now, to the health of the Honorable——" began Goodhare again.

But Sep interrupted him. Glancing restlessly round the room, he laid his hand on the elder man's arm, and whispered hoarsely:

"Don't. Its unlucky."

"And instead of spending our time drinking healths we'd better be deciding what to do with these dangerous little toys, now we've got them," suggested Rees drily. "As long as they remain in their present form the sight of them by an outsider might expose our motives to misconstruction."

The words were scarcely out of his mouth when the door burst open, and the landlady, a rheumatic old woman in a rusty black cap, entered with only that perfunctory knock which is more like a fall against the door in the act of opening it, than a respectful request for permission to enter. Mrs. Williamson was quite taken aback at the sight of the treasures on the table. Luckily for them, the confederates also were so utterly overwhelmed by this unexpected surprise, that no one of them made so much as an instinctive movement as if to hide the jewels.

After a few moments' dead pause, during which the old woman remained blinking at the gems, and the three men felt as if the handcuffs were already on their wrists, Mrs. Williamson, with a short laugh, put all their fears to flight with half a dozen words.

"Well, I never," she said. "What finery to be sure!"

It had not for a moment occurred to this matter-of-fact Londoner that the crowns were "real." Her words suddenly opened the eyes of the three men to a different view of the gold and precious stones before them. Knowing them to be genuine, they had seen them illuminated by the glow with which the consciousness of their value endowed them. Looking at them all at once from the landlady's point of view, they saw that in the weak and murky daylight which came through the dirty window the jewels looked wonderfully little better than theatrical properties. The resourceful Amos hailed this idea with delight. Seizing one of the crowns, he held it over his own head, and asked gaily:

"Well, Mrs. Williamson, what do you think of my crown? You didn't know that I went in for acting, did you? I'm going to play Richard the Third to-night."

"And a very handsome-looking king too, I'm sure, sir. But you should have gone to 'Ales, in Wellington-street, for your crown, begging your pardon for suggesting it. He'd never have sent you such a one as that, with a dirty old piece of velvet in the middle not fit to touch. I've had a actor—not an amateur like you, sir, but one who did it for his living—on my third floor, and he had a much better one than that from 'Ales, much brighter and bigger jewels."

"Well, I must remember that for the next time. I think now this will have to serve my purpose."

"Mrs. Williamson thought they were real at first, I believe," laughed Rees, throwing himself on the sofa.

"Indeed, sir, I did not," said the old woman indignantly. "I've not always been redooced to letting lodgings, and there was a time when I had jewellery of my own, though you mayn't choose to believe it. And I don't suppose now there's many better judges about of what's good than what I am, sir. However, I hadn't come to tell you that, but to know whether I should lay the cloth for dinner?"

"Certainly, and Mr. Goodhare will dine with us to-day," said Rees.

Sep and Rees had each a little room on the second floor, but Goodhare's lodgings were at Westminster. There was too much business to be settled, however, for them to separate for the present. So they ate a hurried meal, had the table cleared, and then very gently, very noiselessly, opened the window and looked out.

The fog was thicker than ever, settling down upon the city for such a night as the three confederates loved. Only a little bit of sky was visible at all from this ground floor room, for the backs of the houses behind came very close, leaving between the two walls of blackened brick nothing but a passage paved with worn and irregular flags. When a good look to right and left had assured the three men that no one was about and that the fog was thick enough to hide them from a chance observer at any of the adjacent windows, one by one they dropped through their own window into the passage, turned to the right, and over the wall at the end into a second and much narrower passage, which ran at right angles to the first, along the backs of the deserted houses which had struck Deborah Audaer with such a sense of poverty and desolation.

The back doors of all these houses were boarded up as carefully as the windows and doors in front. But Rees, who was the first of the three to venture on this errand, stopped at the door of the fourth house, with one strong pull wrenched off the two lowest boards, and crawled through the opening thus made. For the door itself had been taken bodily away. A minute later, Sep, and then Goodhare, had passed through also.

As soon as they were all inside they drew up the displaced boards, which were joined together, fastened them in their place with bolts, and proceeded together along the passage which ran from the back to the front of the house. Without striking a light they felt for and found, about half way along the passage, an opening in the floor which led, by a narrow ladder-staircase, into the cellars.

The first they entered was at the front, underneath that part of the house which had once been a shop. It was very dimly lighted through a rusty grating just below the shop window, and was full of scraps of paper, heaps of dust, and rubbish of the most worthless kind, such as not even the poorest rag-picker would find it worth while to carry away. Behind this miserable and mouldy-smelling cellar was a second, more miserable and mouldy still. It had been sunk some three feet deeper into the earth than the front one, from which it was divided by a brick wall, in which a wooden door had been inserted, artfully painted so as to be undistinguishable, except by an experienced eye, from the brickwork on either side. Into this lower cellar all three men dropped and shut the door behind them.

Then Goodhare struck a light. The cellar was small, and ventilated only by a hole about a foot square in the floor of the back shop above. Immediately under this hole was a small, roughly-made square grate, and above the grate there swung a huge melting-pot. The rest of the furniture consisted of a couple of benches, a dirty table on which was a piece of brown paper containing tools, a large collection of wine and spirit bottles, both empty and full, and a wide, comfortable-looking, old-fashioned couch.

Rees and Sep set to work without delay, extracting the precious stones from their heavy setting with accustomed fingers. In the meantime Amos built up a fire in the rusty grate, and as fast as a piece of gold was deprived of its jewels, he threw it into the melting-pot. While he did so he issued his next instructions to the two younger men.

"We shall have a day or two to work in, boys, because I expect they'll try to recover the things first without raising a hue and cry. Cenarth will know it's life and death to him to get them back quietly. You, Sep, will have to cross to Amsterdam to-night. I'll take care to make up such a parcel as no one shall suspect. You will represent yourself as a merchant of—Tunis, say—who has been trading in South Africa. When you have disposed of as much there as you safely can, go on to Paris, and try—not the big firms—they'll be on the alert by that time—but rich private Americans. Try the swell hotels. Stay at the Grand or the Louvre, and look out for Bertram, the railway millionaire; he's due in Paris in a day or two. With him you may suggest the real source they came from; you needn't give him all particulars. But if you manage well, he'll nibble. And there will be no haggling. Do you understand? Keep your head clear—but you always do when there's work in hand. I must do you that justice."

"Justice!" echoed Sep sulkily. "I shall get a little too much of that before this affair is over, I fancy. There's nothing in what we've done up to now. It might have been done over and over again if the rascals who thought of the Crown jewels before us hadn't remembered the certainty of discovery afterwards. I'm tired of playing cat's-paw. Go to Amsterdam yourself. You're much more like a Tunisian merchant than I am. And you've more nerve. I don't know what's become of mine, but it's gone."

And Sep shivered as he cast round him another of the restless glances which Amos had noticed in him all day. Goodhare looked at him searchingly, and then laid an encouraging hand on his shoulder.

"I'd go with pleasure, my boy, if I could do what is to be done as well as you. But my Greek and Hebrew would not serve me as your knowledge of modern languages serves you; besides, you have been a traveller, and I a stay-at-home, and there is a difference between those two classes which I could not hide."

"Come, Sep, don't make difficulties," said Rees impatiently. "We have all our different departments and separate work. Goodhare organises, I have the chief hand in carrying out——"

"And I do the dirty work," added Sep querulously. "I shall have to go, of course; I know that. But it will be the last time; I feel it. So look out for yourselves."

"What do you mean? You're not going to round on us, I suppose?" said Rees, savagely.

"No, I haven't the spirit to do that, as you know. But I—I've been seen—I'm sure of it. On my way back from that cursed Tower I seemed to see faces peering out of the fog—Charles Cenarth's and Lord St. Austell's. Of course I'll go if you insist, but I tell you it will be a d——d unlucky journey."

His companions laughed at his fears, did their best to raise his drooping spirits, and at last, chiefly by the aid of consoling potations, restored him to something like his old cheerful submissiveness. Then, taking swift advantage of the change in him, they equipped him for his journey with a disguise which Amos had had ready, with clothing, with money, and with a travelling bag with a false bottom, in which, between layers of tissue paper, the stolen jewels were packed. All these preparations being completed, Amos mixed a loving cup, which they all drank solemnly to their usual toast on the eve of one of their nefarious enterprises:

"Success to the Princes of the Fog."

But somehow the old spirit flagged. As the light from the glowing charcoal fire flickered up on their faces, each seemed to see distorting shadows of fear and failure on the features of his companions. They finished the ceremony with unusual haste and in unusual silence, and climbing up out of the damp yet stifling underground retreat, slipped out into the raw air, and getting over the palings unseen in the mist, emerged into Charing Cross-road. Rees and Goodhare accompanied Sep as far as St. Martin's Church, and left him with just time to catch the continental mail train from Charing Cross. Then they returned to Rees Pennant's lodgings.

"For," whispered Amos, as soon as their companion had left them, "I have something for you also to do."

As soon as they were again within closed doors, the older man unburdened himself of his instructions.

"I didn't wish to frighten Jocelyn," he began ominously, "for the lad's turning soft and doesn't need warning to be careful at any time. But there's no denying that this is a dangerous business, the most ticklish thing we've had on our hands yet."

"Yes, of course," assented Rees gloomily.

"So I think we had better get as near the safe side as possible."

He paused.

"Well?" said Rees.

"Now, the best shelter we can get behind is—influence."

"Whose?"

"Lord St. Austell's."

Rees started.

"The man we both hate?"

107

"Why should that prevent our making use of him? Now he can't, in common decency, let me suffer if he can help it. It lies with you to make it equally impossible for him to let you suffer."

"Go on; out with it."

"Become his son-in-law without delay. Marion will jump at you."

Rees moved uneasily.

"I know that. If she were a little less ready, I might be a little more so."

"This is not a time to stick at trifles. You had an appointment with her to-night at a friend's house?"

"Yes, but I can't go—fog's too thick for me to venture out."

"She'll venture, I suppose?"

The young man shrugged his shoulders contemptuously.

"Of course. She'd walk through the Thames to meet me at any time."

"Then your unparalleled devotion must stand even this test. You must meet her to-night and arrange to marry her with as little delay as possible."

Rees made a grimace.

"Can't it be put off until we see how things really turn out?"

"No," answered Amos, decisively, "we can really only reckon on safety for a few hours. You see we were all seen. Our best chance, yours and mine, is to remain where we are, keep perfectly quiet, and trust to Sep's keeping his head; in the meantime we must take all the precautions we can, and yours is—Lady Marion."

Rees got up from his chair with a very sour face.

"All right," he said briefly. "If it's got to be done, here goes."

He ran upstairs to his room without another word, and returned in twenty minutes in evening dress and overcoat, wearing the tired and blasé air which was now no affectation with him. His pale face, curly hair, and great black eyes with dark rings under them, made him look what ladies call "interesting," a fact of which he did not appear to be ignorant.

"Will it do?" he asked, carelessly, as he took up his gloves.

"First-rate," answered Amos, with a nod.

And with much apparent reluctance, part of which was real and part affected, Rees Pennant jumped into a hansom and gave the driver an address in a street near Russell-square.

CHAPTER XVIII.

THROUGH all Rees Pennant's changes of conduct, of manner, of thought, of appearance, Lady Marion Cenarth had remained unswervingly faithful and devoted, brooding over the short notes Goodhare induced him to write to her, with alternate rapture and anxiety; making appointments to meet him at the house of a convenient friend, bearing with his caprices of temper, proud of his tepid sufferance of her vehement adoration, ready at all times, as she repeatedly hinted, to throw away the dignity of her sex and position, and incur all the humiliation and danger of a private marriage. This step, in spite of Goodhare's persuasions, Rees was in no hurry to take. Poor Lady Marion's devotion was perhaps too slavish, too entirely unconcealed, to have been highly valued by any man. It therefore speedily palled upon Rees, who was not only accustomed to feminine adoration, but who had become doubly fastidious since Deborah Audaer's visit to town.

The appearance of the beautiful country girl, with her modest, straightforward manner, and handsome, yet most innocent, eyes, had been like a draught of fresh, sweet air to a man coming out of a chamber foul with asphyxiating gases—not without a certain chilling effect, but refreshing, invigorating, pure—reminding him of the wholesome joys of the life he had left, and contrasting them with the feverish, soul-deadening pleasures of the life he was leading. So that, dropping out of his mind altogether his own shameful conduct on that occasion, he had allowed himself to brood over Deborah's image as that of the angel who—but not before he was tired of it—should lead him back from his exhausting London life to recruit his energies in quiet Carstow.

So that this mandate of Amos Goodhare's to go and marry Lady Marion fell in the midst of his dreams with disconcerting suddenness. Amos had used his craft so well on Rees's weak nature that not all Sep's shrewd observations had been able to shake the young man's confidence in the judgment of the old. Amos thought for him, and Rees acted upon those thoughts with docility, though he constantly protested with a verbal freedom which Goodhare, while permitting, hated him for.

Rees, therefore, did not now stay to ask himself whether Amos had some private motive in this matter of his marriage, but he arrived at the meeting-place in the worst possible temper.

Mrs. Walker, Lady Marion's accommodating friend, was the wife of a city architect, and one of those persons who are ready, by no matter what means, to attach themselves to people of a rank superior to their own. Although exceedingly small, plain, and vulgar she had, by the attractions of a coarse, easy-going good nature and a somewhat startling freedom of speech, secured the equivocal attentions of a young fellow of no brains but of good social position, and it was through him that she had made the acquaintance of Lady Marion Cenarth, who was his own cousin. Mrs. Walker was therefore just the sort of person to be an accommodating friend, and Lady Marion, while inwardly loathing her unrefined manners, was glad to make use of her.

On this particular evening Mrs. Walker had had an appointment to go to the theatre, but the fog having prevented her keeping it, she gave Lady Marion her undesirable companionship, and the two sat in the drawing-room with Francis Cenarth, the brainless one before mentioned; the hostess trying to talk a jargon of fashionable slip-slop, to which Lady Marion who, whatever her faults might be, was not frivolous, turned rudely inattentive ears.

"He's not coming, my dear, that is clear, so I should advise you to give up hope, and look pleasant," whispered Mrs. Walker, as she crossed over to her friend with a cup of tea.

But at that moment a cab stopped at the door, and Lady Marion, with a naïve start and a flushing face, betrayed her hopes. A minute later Rees was in the room.

If Lady Marion was annoyed at the presence of Mrs. Walker, her admirer was unspeakably relieved by it. He drank cup after cup of tea, and bore lightly the chief burden of the conversation, delighted to shorten the inevitable tête-à-tête in which he would have to forswear his liberty and be surfeited with unwelcome caresses. At last, however, the hostess proposed to show her own admirer a picture her husband had just bought, in order to allow the supposed passionate lovers an opportunity of exchanging mutual vows. The two drawing-rooms, which were both furnished with a good taste which seemed at first sight a surprising characteristic of their occupier, ran from the front to the back of the house, and were divided simply by a reed curtain. Mrs. Walker passed through these with Francis Cenarth, and Rees was left to make his proposal. As usual, having let Amos make up his mind for him, Rees was not long in carrying out his instructions when once he and the opportunity stood face to face.

The reed curtain had scarcely ceased to rustle behind his hostess and her companion, when he threw himself into a chair by Lady Marion's side.

"Well, Marion," he said in a rather languid, pretty-pretty manner, "have you any idea why I was so anxious to see you to-night?"

The poor girl flushed with surprise and agitation. Indeed, she had not noticed any great degree of anxiety in her lover's manner. Knowing her own personal disadvantages, with a cankering knowledge that she was lean, high-shouldered, awkward, and altogether without beauty, and regarding Rees with worshipful eyes which even exaggerated his good looks and attractions, she had always been content with very little. Now, therefore, she scarcely dared to think that the goal of her hopes was really reached.

"No, Rees," she stammered, looking at him with sudden, most eloquent shyness, and a bright gleam of excitement in her rather dull blue eyes, "I—I didn't know that you had any particular reason."

"And if I tell you that I have, can you guess what it is?"

"No—no, Rees."

She had scarcely uttered these words when a cab drew up so sharply outside that, in the fog, the horse stepped upon the curbstone, and was got off amid much shouting and clatter. Rees jumped up and looked out from behind the blind to see what had happened. He stepped back muttering an exclamation, with a strange look in his eyes.

"It's the earl," he said briefly.

Lady Marion started to her feet with a cry, and stood for a few moments staring at him vacantly. Then, whispering quickly:

"Behind the curtain—the other room—papa must not see you!" she met Mrs. Walker, just as the latter, hearing a loud and peremptory ring, ran in from the next room.

"It's my father," said Lady Marion.

Mrs. Walker did not notice the girl's tone of alarm. The honor of having an earl in her house, no matter what his errand might be, out-weighed every other thought in her mind. She had only time to draw one deep breath of gratification before the drawing-room door was opened and Lord St. Austell was announced.

He walked in with a firm step and dignified manner—"every inch a nobleman" was the description Mrs. Walker afterwards gave of him. With a curt bend to the lady, who came forward very ready to overflow with an effusive welcome, he asked shortly:

"My daughter is here, I believe, madam?"

"Yes, papa," said a tremulous voice behind him.

He turned and saw Lady Marion standing near the door, with a very white face. Then, with only a glance at her, he again addressed the lady of the house.

"Can I have a few words with my daughter alone, madam?"

Nothing could be more courteous than his words and attitude, nothing more contemptuous than his tone and manner. It was impossible to mistake the fact that he took at a glance the measure, social and moral, of the person he was addressing. No upbraidings, no explanations were necessary. Mrs. Walker retired at once with some incoherent words which sounded like an apology, and the earl turned at once again to his daughter.

"Last week you begged of me," he began at once, without any preface, "two letters from General Wenlock as autographs, you said. Who did you give them to?" No answer. "Was it to Amos Goodhare?"

Another pause.

Then, in a stifled voice, poor Lady Marion answered, "No, papa."

"Who was it to, then?"

He was perfectly quiet. Rees, who was listening, with bated breath, behind the reed curtain, could only just distinguish the words.

Again Lady Marion made no answer.

The earl spoke again, after a short silence, in very measured tone.

"Your uncle Charles will be a ruined man by this time to-morrow unless we find out into what hands those letters have got. They have been used for purposes of forgery."

The girl uttered a low cry and hid her face in her hands.

"Will you tell me now?"

"I cannot."

She lifted a countenance like that of a dead person, staring wildly, blankly, before her.

"Then I know. It was Rees Pennant!"

Lord St. Austell was by no means a dull person when an important occasion arose for the exercise of his wits. He had been told where to find his daughter by a servant who knew better than to say what reason took her to Mrs. Walker's, and until this moment he had not had the least suspicion of her attachment to Rees and her secret correspondence with him. But he had caught sight of a slight, well-formed figure he recognised behind the reed curtain, for neither Rees nor Lady Marion had remembered that a small lamp was burning at the back of the second room. In an instant the earl understood everything. Connecting Amos with the change in Rees, as he had already known how to connect him with the personation of himself at the Tower that day, he felt that he had now more than a clue, and therefore spoke with certainty.

Marion was in despair. She at once began a denial so energetic that Rees, perceiving that the game was up, stepped through the rustling reeds with a grand air.

"It is unnecessary to say more," he said, standing in the centre of the room, conscious even at this moment of the effective picture he made. "I admit that the letters were given to me."

The earl came to the point at once. What were these two, this knave and this fool, that he should spend time and words on them when the honor of his family was at stake?

"Then you know where the jewels are," he said, still in a low voice, but with perceptibly rising excitement. "Put me in the way of finding them to-night, and you may marry my daughter to-morrow."

Rees gave him a low bow.

"Thank you," he said. "You do me too great an honor. For, in the first place, I don't want to marry your daughter; and in the second, the jewels you speak of have already passed out of my reach and out of my knowledge altogether. I wish your daughter a better husband than I should make, the Crown jewels a better keeper than your brother, and yourself a very good evening."

With a low but a very rapid bow, Rees darted out of the room, only just evading the grasp which the earl, beside himself with rage, would have laid upon his coat-collar. In another instant the front door slammed behind him with a noise that echoed through the house, and two minutes later still he was as much lost to the earl in the pitchy blackness of the fog as if he had left the regions of earth.

CHAPTER XIX.

WHILE Rees Pennant and his two confederates in evil were passing an existence of feverish excitement in London, life at Carstow rippled on with the monotony of a brook in a plain. The only break that ever occurred in the quiet uniformity of Deborah's daily duties was on the occasion of Godwin's visits, which had become more frequent of late. He was thinking seriously of "settling down," so he told Deborah soon after Christmas. He now spent every second Sunday at his mother's house, and, by Deborah's imperatively express command, had altogether given up making her his matter-of-fact offers of marriage, and spent much of his time at Carstow, away from the house.

"Settling down?" echoed Deborah, laughing, when he made this announcement. "That seems rather an odd expression to apply to yourself, Godwin. You've never been anything else than settled down. Now you might, with some sense, apply that term to Rees."

"Rees, Rees, Rees," repeated Godwin, impatiently. "You don't mean to say that after all this time, you have Rees as much on the brain as ever."

"'Out of sight' is not 'out of mind' with us women," answered Deborah, didactically.

"Not when you live in the country, perhaps. If you lived in a big town you'd learn better how to rate people at their proper value."

"And you would go up, you think, and poor Rees down?"

"Certainly, if you used the educational advantages of town life as you ought. But to come back to the point—when I say I intend to settle down, I mean to marry. I didn't tell you about it before, because I knew it would distress you."

"Distress me, why?"

"Well, everyone thinks more highly of the prize they've lost. So I knew that you, when you found I was engaged to somebody else, would have some regrets, however transient, at having thrown away your chances."

"You are very good, and in consideration of that goodness, I'll shed all my tears in private."

"But if I don't mind seeing them? If I should *like* to see them?"

"Then I shall know that you are a mere monster of selfish cruelty, and I shall keep them to myself all the more."

"Well, don't you want to know who I'm engaged to?"

"I *do* know."

Godwin looked much astonished.

"To the second Miss Brownlow."

He sat down in the next chair to Deborah, and stared at her in blank amazement.

"But—but you've never seen me with her! I'm perfectly certain that in your presence I've never exchanged half a dozen words with her."

"No, but she is the very girl mamma and I picked out for you, as being admirably suited to you in every way—sensible, practical, straightforward and quite nice-looking enough."

"Quite nice-looking enough for me; I see."

"Now don't be angry. The fact that you've chosen her proves that she *is* nice-looking enough for you. And knowing how sensible you are, and how you always do the right thing, it was quite natural to expect that you would choose the right woman. When are you going to be married?"

"I don't know," answered Godwin, shortly, "it depends on who my wife is."

"What! I thought you said you were engaged!"

"I am—or very near it. But I am going to give you one more chance."

"And Miss Brownlow?"

Godwin shrugged his shoulders.

"She'll suffer less at the loss of such an ordinary admirer as I than she would by gaining such an ordinary husband as I should make—to her."

"And do you think," asked Deborah, looking full at him with an expression of great scorn, "that that would be honorable conduct? You who know what an opportunity of marriage means to a girl in a country town?"

Godwin returned her look very straightforwardly.

"Isn't that rather a low point of view to look at the matter from?"

"It is probably hers."

"Well, that admission condemns you. For I decline to think that the well-being and happiness of a girl whose only aim in existence is to catch a husband by any means she can is of so much consequence as—well, as mine. Is that frank enough?"

Deborah was a little taken aback by this straightforward egotism.

"Then you must logically deny any sort of equality between men and women?"

"I do, emphatically. Women are our superiors or our inferiors, never our equals. And better education for them will not alter this fact; it will accentuate it."

"Now you are running right away from the point, which is this. Is the inequality between the sexes so great that a man may jilt a girl for his own happiness without losing his right to be considered an honorable man?"

"Well, he loses the first freshness of his honor; but if he gets rid of a girl who could be nothing better than his housekeeper, to get one who will be, in the noblest sense of the word, his wife, he gains a great deal more than he loses."

"And if she brings an action for breach of promise?"

"Then she loses the cloak which has so far covered her natural want of delicacy."

"You are as hard and didactic as ever."

"I'm not hard; but I have a few gleams of sense left shining through the mass of cobwebs with which you have filled my head."

"I don't understand the simile."

"Well, I'm in love with you; I love you so much that I'd rather come to you without a rag of honor left than be saluted as the noblest man in the world by any other woman. Just as you, who know that Rees has turned out such a scamp that we daren't inquire into his actions, would think nothing of lowering yourself to the point of forgiving him."

Deborah got up and touched the bell for tea, too much agitated to answer him. Godwin had not only spoken to her with less reserve than ever before, but had looked at her with passion, and finally poured out his words with a vehemence quite in sharp contrast with his accustomed matter-of-fact manner.

"Well," said he, rising quickly and leaning over her as she rang the bell; "do you think more of me now than you did before?"

"No. Less," she answered sharply.

But it was not true. No woman thinks less of a man for letting her into the secrets of his innermost feelings. Godwin retreated, however, without guessing this, and made no further reference to their conversation until the following morning, when he was on the point of starting on his journey back to his work.

"You needn't tell my mother anything about Miss Brownlow," he said hurriedly, in a low voice, with his hat in his hand and his eyes on the floor.

"But why not? I think she would be pleased. Mamma likes her. And poor mamma wants cheering just now."

"Yes; but it might not come off, you know, and then she'd be disappointed. Well, you'll see me again in a fortnight."

"You're more assiduous in your courtship of Miss Brownlow than you were in my case."

"Yes, there's more work to do in getting up the excitement."

"Godwin, I have something serious to say to you about mamma. You know how reserved she is."

"Yes."

"And don't you notice a difference in her from visit to visit."

"I am afraid I do. And I know the reason of it—Rees."

Deborah's voice dropped to an emphatic whisper.

"She is breaking her heart about him."

Godwin began to move restlessly from one foot to the other.

"Well, well; perhaps that sad ignorance is better than full knowledge would be."

Deborah shuddered.

"There is nothing to be done, Godwin, is there?"

He shook his head.

"Not until the prodigal comes back—as he will do sooner or later, to oust the dutiful son," he answered bitterly.

Deborah said nothing to this—did not even look at him—but her cheeks flushed guiltily.

"Well, good-bye, you'll miss your train," she said at last.

"Good-bye," said he curtly.

And he turned abruptly, without again offering to shake hands, and started on his way to the station.

It was true that Mrs. Pennant brooded over the defection of her eldest son. Without having discussed the matter with any one, she knew that there was something discreditable in his mode of life, something which none of the artfully worded suggestions in her own letters could induce him to confess. Belonging, as she did, to that numerous class of women who would allow their sons any latitude and spend their time in efforts, not to reform their darlings, but to shield them, she lived in perpetual terror lest Rees should "get into trouble;" and when, three days after Godwin's confession to Deborah, Lord St. Austell was announced one morning while Mrs. Pennant was taking her breakfast in her bed-room, the old lady sprang up from her chair with an intuitive conviction that this visit concerned her son.

Deborah thought so too. Wishing therefore to spare the old lady as much as she could of any coming shock, she cried out, as Mrs. Pennant hurried towards the door.

"What, mamma, you are surely not going to let Lord St. Austell see *you* in your dressing-gown!"

The old lady stopped. The habits of her life conquered even her impatience for news of her son. Stepping back to the looking-glass and catching sight of her haggard old face and unsmoothed hair, she said:

"You go down, Deborah, and tell his lordship I shall be ready to receive him in ten minutes."

But Deborah thought she could reckon on a good half-hour. She was white and agitated herself when she entered the morning-room, where the earl was standing by the fire. His expression told her that her fears were well-founded.

"I don't know how to break the news to you," he said at once, in a low voice, as they shook hands. "But have you heard anything? You look as if you had."

"Nothing. I have only guessed by your face, and in fact from your coming, so early, so unexpectedly. Mamma guessed too."

"The old lady? She isn't up yet, is she?" asked he anxiously.

"Yes. She will be down in a few minutes."

"Then I must make haste. For I could not meet her. You know it is about—Rees."

"Is he dead?"

"No, unhappily, I might almost say. He is concerned in a stupendous robbery."

Deborah listened with surprising outward calmness. She had expected some calamity of this sort for such a long time that it almost seemed to her that she was hearing old news.

"Is he in the hands of the police?" she asked quietly.

"No. They have not even been informed of the robbery yet, except perhaps unofficially. For the great object is to get the jewels back without noise."

"Jewels?"

"Crown jewels."

Deborah started. She had not expected anything so sensational as that.

"What are you going to do?" she whispered.

"I am going to try home influence, your influence, if you will help us."

"Of course."

"Put on your things." He looked at his watch. "We have twenty-eight minutes before the train starts. No time to lose. If by to-night we are not in the way to recover the jewels we must trust to the police."

Deborah ran to the door, but, with her fingers on the handle, she turned with a white face.

"Mamma!" she whispered, scarcely doing more than form the words with her lips, "she is outside."

She rattled the handle, but still she heard the sound of heavy breathing on the other side. At last, very gently, she opened the door, and found, as she had begun to fear, Mrs. Pennant on her knees, with half-closed eyes, in a kind of fit. The old lady had known that an attempt would be made to keep from her something concerning her son, and had had recourse to eavesdropping to find out the truth.

"I can't go up to London now," said Deborah quietly, but in a tone of despair.

"We will see," said the earl.

Before she could say another word he was out of the house. In five minutes the family doctor had arrived, and in ten minutes Mrs. Kemp, the admiral's widow, was standing by the bed to which her old friend had been carried. It was a stroke of paralysis, the first, and not a very severe one.

Within an hour Mrs. Pennant had recovered sufficiently to remember what she had heard, and to insist on her adopted daughter's going up to town.

By the next train, therefore, Lord St. Austell and Deborah Audaer were on their way to London.

CHAPTER XX.

IN the midst of his anxiety on his brother's account Lord St. Austell was filled with admiration, but rather puzzled, by the entire change in Deborah's manner towards him. Being on old man of the world he was able, as soon as he had done for the time all there was to be done, to ease his mind sufficiently of its burden to enjoy the idea of a long tête-à-tête with the beautiful girl. When he asked her if he should have the compartment reserved, she made no objection. When he loaded her with little attentions, and began to assume his most fascinating manner, she thanked him smilingly, but still showed none of the rather distant timidity with which she had formerly treated his advances. He grew more and more anxious to know the reason of this change.

"I did not think, Miss Audaer, at this time yesterday that I should ever have the pleasure of a journey in your society."

"No indeed, nor did I," said Deborah simply.

"In fact, at one time I was afraid that I had had the misfortune to come under the ban of your displeasure."

"Oh no, how could you, when you were so kind to Rees?"

"Yet even your fondness for Rees would never before induce you to come up to London with me to find out how he was getting on."

Deborah said nothing to this. After a short pause Lord St. Austell went on:

"So that, while I am delighted to find that the—shall we call it—prejudice under which I labored in your eyes has broken down, I am at the same time at a loss to account for the change which has made me so happy."

"Are you really?" asked Deborah with surprise, turning towards him eyes full of intelligence and sincerity. "I should have thought a man of your experience would have understood it so easily."

There was no quality of his to which the earl would not rather have heard her allude than to his experience, suggesting, as it did, the years which had brought it. However, he had a great deal too much tact and shrewdness to betray his feeling on the subject.

"I confess," he said, "that long and varied as my experience has been, your charming sex still has surprises for me. Will you explain the reason of the altered light in which you regard me?"

"There has been no alteration. It is simply this: You asked me to accompany you to London this morning with the definite object of trying to do you a service. In those circumstances, unless I am much mistaken in you, a girl might safely trust herself in your care from here to Japan."

The girl's spirit and modesty took the old *roué* by storm. It was such a deft and graceful appeal to all that was best in the traditions of his not very worthy school, that this particular girl was indeed, after making it, an almost sacred object in his eyes. He leaned back in his seat in the carriage, regarding her with admiration more respectfully than before.

"What a strangely different world this would be," he said at last, "if only half the women in it possessed your divine attribute of common sense!"

"Perhaps there are some divine attributes lacking in the men, too," suggested Deborah demurely.

"That is more than likely. But who, that knows anything about him, would expect divinity in such a creature as a man?"

"Not I, for one," answered Deborah, with simple sincerity which was rather startling.

"And it's rather hard, isn't it, that such commonplace, tainted wretches as we are, should expect such moral perfection in our helpmates."

Deborah paused a few moments, and then answered thoughtfully:

"I don't think so. Surely it is better that one-half the world should be good than that none should be. And if a man can't be good himself, it is at least something that he can admire goodness in his wife and wish for a good influence around his children."

The earl was much interested.

"There," said he, with excitement, "is the sensible way of looking at it. What a wife you'd make?"

"Yes," said Deborah, quietly, "to a good husband."

"But I understood you to say——"

"That a man should choose a good mother for his children. But I think also that a woman should choose a good father for hers."

"And you would be very hard to please?"

"Very."

"But don't you know that most women prefer a man not too utterly immaculate?" suggested the earl, gently.

"That is because they hope to reform him."

"And—stop me at once if you think I am getting impertinent—but have you never, never entertained any idea of the sort?"

Deborah blushed, but she turned to answer him very frankly.

"Yes, I have. I wanted very badly to reform Rees Pennant. And that set me thinking what sort of a thing such a reform could be. And then I began to doubt my own powers."

"And you decided to give him up?"

"No, oh no. But I saw that it would need a great deal of love on the man's side as well as on the woman's to bring such a reform about."

"And had you not in the meantime met some one who—well, who insisted on occupying a corner in your thoughts?"

Deborah started.

"Oh, no; at least——." She hesitated in some confusion.

The earl laughed softly.

"Ah, you are a very woman after all. I was beginning to be afraid you were rather too superior to our poor common clay."

"But you are quite wrong if you think——"

"I don't think anything; I never did. I have been a soldier, you know, not a philosopher. I can act, you see; I could run down to Carstow to fetch you; but having done so, I have for the time given up all thought about our errand, and the numerous difficulties this business has thrown me into."

"Indeed!" said Deborah gravely, "I can't think about it clearly; it has come upon me like a misfortune which one has dreamed about all night and which happens in the daytime."

Lord St. Austell shivered, and Deborah saw that his face had turned quite grey, and that his eyes moved restlessly, as if trying to escape the sight of some haunting object. He opened one of the pile of papers he had hastily bought at the station, and asked her opinion upon one of the public topics of the day. But that his mind was more burdened by the object of their journey than he chose to confess was proved by a remark into which he burst quite abruptly after a long silence.

"This young scamp Rees has a wonderful fascination about him. He has bewitched one of my own daughters. I caught them together last night at the house of some miserable little snob."

"Lady Marion?" said Deborah quietly.

"What? You have heard?"

"Oh, that has been well known for a long time."

"To every one but me, I suppose?"

"I should think so."

"Well, your confession that a woman can become disgusted with even a worthless man gives me hope."

"I did not speak for every woman, remember," said Deborah warningly.

Her caution was justified. At Paddington, waiting for the train from Carstow, stood poor Lady Marion, leaner, more hatchet-faced than ever, in a long cloak and a shabby black hat, looking old enough for her own mother. Deborah saw her first, and jumping quickly out of the carriage, went up to her. The poor thing looked at the handsome girl before her with angry eyes, and would have turned her back and walked on. Deborah was not to be daunted.

"We have come to try and save Rees," she whispered, following her.

Lady Marion turned quickly.

"To save him! Ah, yes, *you*," she added immediately, in a bitterly envious tone. "He loves you."

"Well, if you care for him, surely the great thing is that he should be saved," urged the other persuasively.

Lady Marion had stopped reluctantly, and she now looked everywhere but at Deborah's beautiful face.

"But papa, what does he say?"

Before her companion could answer, Lord St. Austell was beside them. He looked coldly and sternly at his daughter.

"Come down here, out of the crowd," said he. "I wish to speak to you."

He took her arm and led her down the platform to the almost deserted end, which is, morning and evening, piled with huge milk cans going and returning between the London dairies and the country. Deborah followed them at a long distance, and waited. The earl addressed his daughter very coldly.

"What is the meaning of this exhibition. You promised me, when I took you home last night, that you would remain there."

"I couldn't papa, I couldn't," sobbed the girl.

"What have you come here for?"

"To tell you that I love him, and that if you don't let him off I shall kill myself and let everybody know why. You don't believe me!" the poor distracted creature continued passionately.

"I do. I could believe anything of such an idiot," said her father contemptuously. "You have seen him, I suppose, this morning?"

"No. I don't know where he lives."

"Ah, he was afraid of your worrying him even at his rooms, evidently." And he uttered an exclamation of disgust. "Now go home. Nothing is further from my thoughts than punishing Rees. I would not even give him a fool for a wife."

He led her, without too much gentleness, through the station, put her in a hansom, and gave the driver the address of his home.

Then, with a laconic caution that she had better remain at home and keep quiet, he turned his back upon her and went in search of Deborah, whom he found just inside the doors, wearing a rather sad face.

"I wish that foolish girl of mine had a little of your sense," said he, as he helped Deborah into a hansom and got in after her.

"She is the ideal faithful woman, though."

"Yes, because she has no beauty."

They drove on in silence to the lodgings in St. Martin's-lane, where, in answer to their inquiries, they were told that Mr. Pennant still lived; then they were ushered into the little back room, which Deborah remembered, and, finding that Rees was not there, they said they would wait. Mr. Pennant's hours were very uncertain, the old landlady, who opened the door herself, said; and as he scarcely ever had a meal at home, and always let himself in with a latch-key, she could give very little information about his movements. Both Mr. Pennant and Mr. Jocelyn, she mentioned, as if it was no uncommon occurrence, had slept out last night.

"Jocelyn!" repeated Lord Austell, turning to Deborah.

"It must be Sep, Mrs. Kemp's nephew," answered she.

"We will wait," repeated he. "If you should meet either of them on their way in, don't tell them any one is here. We want to surprise them."

"Very well, sir," said Mrs. Williamson. Then she continued, with a smile, "If Mr. Goodhare should call, sir, I suppose you would wish him told that his brother is inside?"

Lord St. Austell started.

"Brother!" he repeated sharply.

"Lor', yes, sir, I saw the likeness in a minute!"

The earl glanced in the looking-glass over the mantelpiece, and laughed with an effort.

"No," he said. "Let him in, but don't let him know I'm here."

"Very well, sir."

She left the room, and the earl turned to Deborah in great agitation.

"Now do you know who is the prime mover in all this?" he asked, almost fiercely, when the door closed.

"Amos Goodhare," she answered quietly. "He has been Rees's evil genius for the last eighteen months."

"And mine for a much longer time than that. But," he added gloomily, after a pause, "I would have avoided meeting him if I could. It can do no good. He is a rascal, but I cannot charge him, and he knows it."

He was silent for some time, pacing up and down the little room, listening intently to every sound, glancing from time to time at his watch impatiently, while the gloom upon his face constantly increased.

"Perhaps none of them will come," suggested Deborah.

"Yes, they will; at any rate *he* will," said the earl. "When I am highly strung, as I am to-night, I can feel a misfortune approaching. And this man has always brought misfortune to me. Don't smile, my dear girl. When you have reached my age, you will believe, at any rate somewhat, in portents."

But Deborah was not smiling. There was something more of solemnity, something more of a kindly dignity, in the earl's manner, as the afternoon wore slowly on. She began to believe, as she watched the change which was creeping over him, and turning him, as it were, from the genial carpet knight into the soldier ready for battle, that they were, indeed, as his

124

presentiment told him, on the eve of some great calamity, which would overshadow even the anxieties from which they were suffering.

The dark afternoon was merging into evening, and the fire had been allowed to sink very low, when, at last, there was a sound of turning of a latch-key in the outer door. The earl, who had been resting for a moment in a chair by the dying fire, with his head in his hands, sat up and signed to Deborah to keep still on the little sofa where she was sitting.

Before she could guess his purpose they both heard a very light tread in the hall outside, the door opened noiselessly, and a man, not at first distinguishable in the darkness, crept into the room like a shadow.

Then by his height, and his stealthy movements, they knew him to be Amos Goodhare.

CHAPTER XXI.

WHEN Amos Goodhare entered the little sitting-room, Deborah was sitting on a sofa, so far back in the black shadow that she knew it was impossible for him to see her. But Lord St. Austell was sitting so far forward in the arm-chair that the faint glow of the little fire shone upon him. Nevertheless, Amos behaved exactly as if he saw no one.

The window was to the left of the door, and only four or five steps from it. He crossed the narrow space with a very soft tread, and throwing open the window, which he did quickly, but without the least noise, descended on the stone flags outside, and, turning to the right, disappeared quickly in the darkness.

Lord St. Austell sprang up from his seat, ran to the window, and strained his eyes to follow him. He had his hand on the sill to jump out after him, when he felt Deborah's touch upon his sleeve.

"Lord St. Austell," she whispered, "don't on any account follow that man alone. He is dangerous."

The earl turned impatiently. He was at all times physically fearless.

"My dear girl, don't be alarmed, these men have nothing to fear and everything to hope from me. By this time they must have found it practically impossible to dispose of the stolen property, and must be in hourly dread of the police. Now, I can hush up the whole affair if they will restore the jewels."

Deborah was still holding his sleeve with no uncertain grip, and she spoke in a low but very decided tone:

"It is not that, but Amos Goodhare has a grudge against you, I am sure of it."

"No reasonable one, I assure you."

By this time the girl was clinging to both his arms, almost struggling with him to prevent his carrying out his purpose.

"What does that matter," she cried, vehemently. "Was a prejudice ever the weaker for being unreasonable? I tell you he saw you and pretended not to, in order to lure you to follow him. You don't know where he's gone, and what accomplices he may have waiting in that nest of dirty courts and passages out there. Get police assistance before you try to find him."

"Confound the girl!" muttered Lord St. Austell savagely, as at last, not without the exercise of something like violence, he got partially free from her clinging hands. "You've made me miss him!"

Deborah let him go at once, with an exclamation of relief.

"That's all right!"

He had already got half out of the window, when suddenly he drew back and came to her. She was sitting by the table leaning her head on her hand.

"I beg your pardon, Miss Audaer," said he, most contritely with the ring of sincere feeling in his voice, as he felt in the obscurity for her hand, which she gave him at once. It was cold and trembling. "My dear girl, I hope I have not hurt you—for heaven's sake, tell me I have not!" he cried with much concern.

"No, you have not," she answered in a hoarse and broken voice. "But I am beginning to feel what you feel—that some dreadful thing is going to happen—that that man's presence brings harm."

"Well, I choose to think that your presence counteracts it, for you are a good, brave girl. Now, child, I want you to wait here for me, and if Rees should come, use your influence with him. I am going to use mine with Amos."

"You are—really?"

"Really. Good-bye for the present."

Deborah was in so excited a state that even the haste with which he added those last three words, "for the present," seemed to her portentous. She listened with straining ears to the last sound of his footsteps as he trod the uneven stones in the direction Amos had taken.

As in the case of most "presentiments," Lord St. Austell's vague foreboding was the result chiefly of very clear and distinct knowledge. He knew very well that his personator at the Tower on the previous day could be no other than Amos Goodhare, between whom and himself there had alway existed a dislike, all the stronger for having been most decently veiled. There was a likeness in the temperament and disposition of the two men as marked as their outward resemblance to each other, and this likeness accentuated their difference of social position, and so increased the mistrust of the one, and the hatred of the other. What treatment, then, could the earl hope to receive at the hands of a man who hated him, who had just proved himself to be an audacious and unprincipled scoundrel, and who held all the cards in his own hands. Lord St. Austell had not the least fear of personal violence; in his younger days he had proved a brave and a lucky soldier, and he would have felt reassured rather than alarmed if he had thought that the matter would be decided by any sort of physical encounter. What he feared was that Goodhare would absolutely refuse to come to terms, would stubbornly affect ignorance of the whole affair, in which case the career of his brother Charles, keeper of the regalia, would be ruined.

As he picked his way over the stones, under the eaves of the outer buildings which had grown up between the old houses, with the raindrops dripping down upon him, and his feet slipping from time to time, with a little splash, into the pools and rivulets in the uneven pavement, he debated which price he should have to pay for the information he wanted.

But he never came near the true one.

He was brought to a standstill, in the midst of his cogitations, by a low brick wall. He was a tall man and he could see over it. He saw the backs of the deserted houses on the left, and a passage running behind them. At the back door of the fourth house a man was standing, who came forward quickly, peering into the darkness. When he was close to the wall he said:

"I beg your pardon. Can you oblige me with a light?"

"Certainly, Amos."

"Your lordship! Is it possible? What can you be doing here?"

"I was looking for you."

"For me! You do me too much honor. But what am I to do? I feel at present rather under a cloud, and, to confess the whole truth, I am in hiding from the police. You know, your lordship, since you threw me over, I have always been an unlucky man."

He spoke in his old tone of almost fawning respect, and his last words conveyed a reproach uttered with tender melancholy. Lord St. Austell's hopes rose.

"Perhaps I can get you out of the police difficulty, Amos, and perhaps you can help me in return," he said in the low voice in which their colloquy had been conducted from the beginning. "Can't you take me somewhere where we can talk. I'm standing with my feet in a pool of water, and with more of the same exhilarating liquid meandering down my back from a broken waterspout over my head."

"Well, I really don't know what to do," said Amos, in apparent confusion. "I've a wretched den on this side of the wall where I hide myself, but it's not the sort of place I could take your lordship into."

"But I give you my word my lordship would prefer anything to his present position."

With a shamefaced effort, Amos apparently made up his mind.

"Come then, my lord, if you will. At any rate, you'll see what straits I'm reduced to."

Something in the man's tone rang false, and Lord St. Austell noticed it. But he did not hesitate. There were notches in the wall which would have made the climbing an easy matter to a less athletic man than he still was, and although he remarked good-humoredly that he had hoped his climbing days were over, he got over without the least difficulty, and followed Amos up the passage.

"Dreary hole this," he exclaimed, glancing up at the deserted houses with their blank, nailed-up windows, and at the cold reflection of a distant gaslamp on the wet pavement at the other end of the passage. Big drops of rain-water splashed down from the broken roofs, and little streams trickled into the passage from bent and rusty water-pipes. "But I should have thought these deserted houses would be just the sort of place the police would keep an eye on."

"I believe they think they are too obviously suitable a hiding-place, and that the fear of a chance inspection would keep poor vagabonds away. I have had an occasional rattle at my shutters from a passing bobby when I have been keeping close, but I have never been disturbed in any other way."

Amos was standing by the door of the fourth house. Bending down, he drew away the lower part of the boarding with which it was nailed up. "I'm afraid your lordship will have to stoop," said he.

As Lord St. Austell instantly bent down to creep through the opening, the face of the other man underwent a sudden change. His features became convulsed with fury, and he drew up his right arm as if the impulse to take advantage of his companion's stooping position was irresistible. The next moment he had controlled himself, and following the earl into the house, he drew up the boards behind them.

It was quite dark inside the passage of the house.

"You go first, Amos," said Lord St. Austell; and he leaned back against the wall for Goodhare to pass him.

"You don't mind going down a floor lower, do you, my lord? I daren't strike a light till we get below the street level."

"Do you take refuge in the cellar then?"

"Your lordship will allow that it is better than a police cell. This way. Shall I go first? Mind how you come. It's only a ladder."

Lord St. Austell followed without hesitation, but he was not so dull as to ignore the fact that his errand was becoming more dangerous than he had expected. He followed to the first cellar, to which a faint light penetrated through a grating below what had once been the shop window. Goodhare, after listening for a few moments to be sure that no tread of a passer-by was audible on the stone pavement outside, pushed open a door on the right and climbed down into a lower cellar which was as much overheated as the upper one was too cold. The ruddy glow of a fire was seen at once on floor and ceiling, and a gust of air hot as the breath of a furnace, seemed almost to sear the wet, cold faces of the two men as they entered.

"Good heavens! I shall never be able to stay down here," exclaimed the earl, stepping back from the huge square iron grate, like the cage of an ancient beacon, which stood in the middle of the floor, and in which blazed an enormous fire.

"Oh, you will manage it as long as I want to keep you," said Amos, quietly.

He drew the door close and made it fast with a rough bolt, while Lord St. Austell examined the cellar in which he found himself, which Amos not inaptly termed a den.

There was no boarding on the floor, nothing but the rough earth. The walls were only bricked in about half-way down, as if the cellar had been dug out after the house was built. A piece of sacking on the floor, two benches, a dirty sofa, and deal table covered with tools and lumber, formed all the furniture. The earl looked attentively at a huge melting-pot which stood before the fire.

"That," said Goodhare, "was what the gold crowns from the Tower were melted in."

The coolness with which he said this caused Lord St. Austell to look round at his companion. He was startled by the change in him. Instead of the stooping, lean librarian, with the shabby coat and cringing manner, he saw a well-dressed, dignified man, with trim grey beard—the counterpart of himself. One great difference there was between them, one only. The earl's eyes looked out upon the world with the cynical and languid interest of a man who has tasted and tired of every human pleasure; those of his companion glowed with the ferocity of a wild beast interrupted in a meal of human flesh.

"Why, Amos, rascality seems to agree with you!" exclaimed St. Lord Austell.

Goodhare laughed harshly.

"Rascality is perhaps too strong a word, as your lordship will perhaps allow when I point out one particular feature of the transactions in which I have lately been engaged. I began, as perhaps you have not yet heard, by taking a little sum that was lying idle on your lordship's property at Carstow. It was in old-fashioned gold, but I managed, with some difficulty, to get it converted into the current coin of to-day."

The two men were standing one on either side of the blazing fire which shot up golden flames and threw a lurid brightness on both faces. There was no other light in the cellar.

Lord St. Austell perceived now that he was in a trap, but no one could have guessed his thoughts from the stolidly calm expression of his face.

"Yes," he said, very quietly. "It is the first I had heard of it. Go on."

"When that little provision was exhausted, I took to the calling of gentlemanly footpad. Before you condemn me, if you look back on the street robberies of the past winter, you will do me the justice to remember that the first was committed on your own person and the rest on those of your intimate friends."

"I don't see how that excuses you."

"I will make it clear to your lordship by-and-bye. Last of all, when my funds had sunk so low that it needed a bold stroke to restore them, I helped myself, with the aid of my friends, to part of the jewels kept in the tower, of which your brother is custodian. Do you see the connection?"

"Of course I see that you seem to have had me always for choice as the victim of your malpractices."

"And you cannot yet see why, my lord?" asked Goodhare, with a panting ferocity which he scarcely now took the trouble to veil.

"No. Except that you are a d——d ungrateful beast, biting by preference the hand that fed you."

"Could your lordship give me a list of your benefactions to me?" asked Goodhare, glaring across at him over the smoke and flame of the fire.

"Well I gave you the post of librarian at Llancader, until I found you taking advantage of the position to rob me of MSS., which, as I see, you knew how to use."

"And did I not earn my pay? Was I idle, drunken, dissolute?"

"Certainly not. You were an ideal librarian, and I respected you for it."

"Respected me for repressing every instinct of my nature, every passion which you were freely indulging! I should think so."

"Our positions were not the same: I could not alter that fact."

"Did you do all for me that my father—and yours—on his death-bed desired that you should do?"

The earl looked uneasy.

"I did all that a man is ever expected to for an illegitimate half-brother," said he evasively. "If I had been a Quixote I couldn't have given up my title to you. The law would not allow it."

"But you could have given up Llancader, as my father, when he was dying, told me you would do."

The earl flushed a little.

"He should have made that provision by will if he wished it attended to. I could not be expected to dismember the property. I am not a rich man, as you know. For my position I'm a poor one. I never have a thousand pounds to spend as I choose."

"Not when your wines and women have all been paid for, I dare say."

"Why sneer? I never knew you cared for those things. You were always for books, books. And a studious man is supposed to be virtuous."

"Why? Is every thought holy that is printed and bound up in morocco? Through your father's dishonesty to my mother and yours to me, I have had to pass the best years of my life in revelry of the imagination only. And so I whetted an appetite for pleasure which I have only just begun to satisfy as yours is exhausted."

The earl felt for the first time in his life an impulse of fear; there was something scarcely human, something ghoulish, in the face before him. The eyes seemed to shoot flames through the fire-smoke.

"I am getting tedious, my lord," continued Goodhare, with mock respect, after a short pause, during which the two men watched each other warily. "Let us sum up the situation. Your father and mine, an unmarried man, deceived my mother, a country lawyer's daughter, by a mock marriage. He took her away to North Wales, and kept her there in privacy, on goodness knows what wretched plea. I was their son—his eldest son. She knew who he was; she thought I was his heir. I was fourteen before, in that out-of-the-way place, we learnt that he had married a woman of his own rank. Then the truth came out. My mother was broken-hearted, and did not live through the year. I was brought up a gentleman and left a beggar. Then, with stupendous generosity you gave me office as librarian—to close my mouth. And all your favors you gave to Rees Pennant, whom for that reason I have ruined. And so I lived near enough to hear the vices condoned in you which in me would have been condemned; to see a beautiful girl repulse my honorable advances with as much horror as she did your dishonorable ones. And yet my mother was a better woman than yours, and *I* am the eldest son."

"But you are mad! Can I help the law?"

"Can I respect it? Let us be logical. You are the eldest son above ground, in the daylight, by right of the law. I am the eldest son down in the earth, from which I took my birthright. And so here, down in the earth, I take my revenge on the law and on you!"

With a spring he leapt over the iron grate, in which the fire now burnt with a steady red glow. Seizing Lord St. Austell by the throat before the earl had the least intimation of his purpose, Goodhare, with a growling noise like a wild beast, twisted him and flung him down on to the red-hot coals. Before his victim had time for more than one struggle, one shout for help, Amos had torn open his waistcoat, and plunging a large claspknife between his ribs, stabbed him to the heart.

With a sigh of fiendish satisfaction, he threw the body, the clothes of which were in a blaze, on to the floor, and wrapping it tightly in the matting, extinguished the flames. Then, unbolting the door, he dragged the ghastly burden across the rough floor, and lifting it, not without difficulty and with an exclamation of disgust, into the upper cellar, he rolled it into a corner with a series of sharp kicks. Striking a match, he cast one more look, full of a thirsty, savage delight, at the staring eyes and mouth distended with horror; then, turning lightly on his heel, he threw away the match, and taking a bottle carefully from a rough wine-bin which stood in one corner, he climbed down into the inner cellar, took a corkscrew from his pocket, opened the bottle lovingly, and, pouring himself out a tumblerful, drank it off with great enjoyment.

CHAPTER XXII.

MEANWHILE, Deborah had suffered much more from gloomy anticipations than the unfortunate Lord St. Austell. She opened the window wide, in spite of the rain and the cold, and putting her head out, listened and watched eagerly for his return.

Half an hour had passed, and her anxiety had reached fever pitch, when the door of the room was opened very slowly. Catching sight of a woman's figure in the gloom, the intruder tried to retreat. But Deborah, who was no fussy young woman, and who was getting tired of mysteries, rushed to the door and kept it shut.

"I know who you are," she cried. "You're Sep Jocelyn. And you shall not go until you have told me everything I want to know."

Sep, in a trembling voice, was trying to silence her throughout the whole of this speech.

"Sh-sh," he whispered as she finished. "Do you want to get me into trouble, perhaps have me murdered! Where's"—and his voice sank still lower—"where's Goodhare?"

"I don't know. He went out through that window some time ago. Do you know where he is gone?"

"It's better not to ask too many questions here, Miss Audaer. Where's Rees?"

"I don't know. I haven't seen him. I want to see him."

"Have you come to see Rees, Miss Audaer?" asked Sep, in a weak, mistrustful voice.

"I will tell you everything when you have lit the gas," said she, struck by the fear in his tones. "Have you any matches about you?"

Very unwillingly Sep produced a box, which Deborah took from him. As soon as the gas was alight she turned to look at him, and surprised a furtive glance towards the door. Before he had time to follow his evident inclination, she put her arm through his and drew him down on to the sofa beside her. Sep never resisted anybody, so of course he yielded like a lamb to her.

"And now," she said, looking him full in the face, "what is the matter with you?"

"Nothing," stammered Sep, glancing quickly at her, and then avoiding her eyes.

The answer was absurd. With his wan face, wrinkled and furrowed by deadly anxiety and fear, and marked with black streaks of smoke and fog, his bloodshot, swollen eyes, his quivering lips, and the trembling fits which from time to time seized his limbs, Sep Jocelyn had evidently something very seriously the matter with him.

"You are cold," said Deborah gently.

"I am always cold."

"Have you just returned from a journey?"

Sep started, and began to tremble so violently that Deborah, with her wits on the alert, began to have an inkling of the truth.

"Listen, Sep," she said in a low, earnest voice. "I know the trouble you and Rees are in. It is through that man Goodhare, I feel sure."

"Sh-sh," interrupted Jocelyn, glancing around him fearfully.

"I've come to get you all out of it. If you will tell me where the jewels are, I can promise you that nothing will ever be heard of the business. And if you will come back to Carstow with me, I can promise that your aunt, who misses you most dreadfully, will take you back to her arms without a word of reproach."

"Oh, no; she couldn't now. You don't know—I can't tell you; but it's too late. The next shelter I get will be a prison."

Deborah was shocked. He was altogether broken down, a mere wreck, a shivering, quaking creature, broken-nerved, bemuddled, helpless.

"Lord St. Austell's influence will keep you out of prison."

"Lord St. Austell!" Sep started violently. "Why, he's the very last person to help us. He has no end of grudges against us, if he only knew."

"He does know, but the career of his brother Charles and the honor of his family outweigh everything with him. You see, if the loss of part of the regalia were made known, there would be a public outcry, and his brother would be disgraced. Now, Sep, what interest have I in the matter except yours and Rees Pennant's?"

"Rees's! Yes, that is true," he muttered.

"Well, then, trust your secret to me. You were sent away with the jewels to dispose of them, were you not?"

Sep admitted this with a half-involuntary nod, not looking at her.

"Where?"

"To Amsterdam."

"But the jewels were only stolen yesterday, and you are back already!"

"I didn't go. I lost heart. I was afraid. I fancied I was followed." And he cast another hunted look around him. "And now I daren't meet Goodhare. And yet—I don't know where to go. So I sneaked back here—to wait—till I'm taken."

"No! Your instinct guided you back to be saved," cried Deborah, in reassuring tones. "You have the jewels with you now?"

"No-o," stammered Sep.

"Oh yes, you have," said she, confidently. "Now, trust them with me, and Goodhare need not know at present that you have not taken them to Amsterdam."

"But where shall I go?"

"Go back to your aunt at Carstow, and she'll nurse all those worried lines out of your face again."

"But I daren't; I'm ashamed to," objected the poor wretch.

"Then go away and hide yourself somewhere for to-night, and be at Paddington to-morrow at twelve, and you shall go down with me."

"And Rees, what about Rees?" asked Sep, who although he had lost most of his old enthusiasm about his friend, still retained the remains of a dogged and not very reasonable devotion to him.

"You don't think I should forget him," said Deborah, gravely.

"Of course not," he answered, hastily. "You will get him out of the scrape too?"

"Certainly."

"But there are so many other scrapes behind this one!"

"I think I can get them all hushed up."

"But then there's Goodhare," whispered Sep, with a shudder. "He'll have us both back if he wants to!"

"I think he will find it expedient to keep out of the way for the future. Now come, we haven't much time."

She held out her hand, assuming a tone of greater confidence than she felt; for she feared that at the last moment Sep might decline to part with the treasure entrusted to him. However, he looked at her outstretched hand, and then, irresolutely, tremblingly drew out from a pocket of his coat first one flat packet, and then another.

Deborah could scarcely refrain from snatching them, or keep her fingers from quivering, as she took them and hid them in the front of her own dress, under her mantle. Sep felt a-trembling as soon as he had given them up, and buried his face in his hands.

"And now," said she, softly, "I must find Lord St. Austell. He went out at that door, following Goodhare."

Sep started up wildly. "Following Goodhare!" he almost shouted. Then, sinking his voice to a hoarse whisper, he stammered out: "You musn't hope anything from Lord St. Austell, then. If Goodhare took him where I expect he did, he would never let him out alive. Goodhare hates him, and he is more devil than man!"

Deborah rose quickly and quietly and opened the door into the yard.

"Take me to this place at once," said she.

Remonstrance with her was useless. With staggering steps Sep accompanied her along the outer passage.

CHAPTER XXIII.

DEBORAH had scarcely got outside the door when she perceived that something more than moral force would be wanted to keep Sep Jocelyn up to the simple task she wished him to perform. The mere thought of intruding unbidden upon Amos Goodhare caused him so much trepidation that she was able to measure the awful extent of the influence the old man had established over the younger ones. When, therefore, Sep had stopped and hesitated half-a-dozen times, she put her hand through his arm and gently urged him forward.

"You had better go back; let me take you back," he whispered, afraid of the strength of her compelling will.

"Not until you have shown me Goodhare's hiding-place, and I have assured myself that Lord St. Austell is safe," she answered firmly.

Sep took a few steps forward with a groan, and stopped short in some relief a couple of feet from the wall at the turn in the passage.

"You'll have to come back now," he whispered; "and I'll try to find out another way round. You can't get over this wall."

"Can't I?" said the country girl contemptuously. "You go first and just give me a hand on the other side."

He obeyed very reluctantly, and he scarcely got over the wall himself when the athletic young girl was by his side. After that, with a sort of dismal acquiescence in the fact that she must have her own way, he led her without further pause to the door of the house which they had made their hiding-place.

Here at last for a moment the girl's brave spirit seemed to fail her. For Sep removed the lower boards of the door noiselessly, and she saw that the house was as black as night inside, and felt the hot fumes of stifling smoke which, coming up through the hole made in the floor of what had once been the back-shop, spread slowly through the whole house, and escaped, through what cracks and crevices it could find, into the open air.

Sep snatched at the opportunity of persuading her to go back.

"Listen," he whispered. "Can't you hear him singing to himself down there?"

Deborah bent forward, and caught certain fitful, crooning sounds, which, rising from time to time to a loud, savage note, made her shiver.

"He sings like that when he has done some diabolical thing," Sep went on. And Deborah heard his teeth chatter. "It would not be safe for you to go near him now."

"But Lord St. Austell! What can have become of him?" asked Deborah with a sudden impulse of alarm stronger than any she had felt yet.

"Well, you can't help him, anyhow," said Sep shuddering.

137

"And Rees?"

Sep did not answer. They were inside the house now, listening to that terrible crooning.

"I must find out what has happened—what is going on," said Deborah suddenly, with decision.

"You can't see anything unless you go down into the first cellar," said Sep, sulkily. "And then, if he heard you go, or saw you through the door, it would be all up with you."

"Won't you come down with me?"

He hesitated, and then said pettishly, "Why can't you come back?"

"I can't till I am sure that no harm has happened to Lord St. Austell. Will you come!"

"I suppose so—if you won't be persuaded," said Sep, sullenly.

It was easy to descend without noise, as every precaution to deaden sound had been taken by the three confederates. The ladder was fixed quite firmly, and the rungs of it were covered with felt. Deborah went down first, and waited at the bottom of the ladder for Sep, not knowing which way to move in the darkness. But he did not come. She did not dare to call to him, and while she was debating with herself whether she should creep up the ladder again and shame him into accompanying her, a very faint sound above told her that he had broken faith and gone back, leaving her to face alone whatever danger might be awaiting her.

Her first impulse on making this discovery was indignation, not with the trembling wretch who had failed her, but with herself for her own folly in trusting him. Then immediately she set about devising what she could do. She heard a cork drawn in the lower cellar, the door of which was shut, and it seemed to her that the weird, droning sound which Amos Goodhare was making grew gradually louder. Was Lord St. Austell hiding somewhere, on the watch like herself, she wondered. Her eyes were getting accustomed to the gloom, and she now perceived, some way to the left, a faint light from above. Moving very cautiously in that direction she perceived that there was a boarded-up-window, and that a few rays of what murky daylight was left filtered through the cracks from a grating above.

As she crossed the floor her boot struck against a couple of boards that were lying there, and made a little clatter. Instantly the crooning in the next room stopped, and Deborah heard sounds as of a seat pushed back. She had time to get close to the wall under the boarded window, and to crouch down, when the door was pushed open, and against a ruddy glow of fire-light she saw the figure of Amos Goodhare.

She kept quite still.

"Rees!" called he, not loud but imperatively. A pause. He repeated the name savagely. Then, between his teeth, he muttered, "D—n the young whelp," and took a few steps into the room.

Deborah could hear her own heart beating.

But Goodhare had not found her out. The next moment she heard the clank of glass, and as he returned to the lower cellar she saw that he carried a bottle of wine under his arm. This time he pulled the door after him, but it rebounded a little way and stood ajar. After a few more minutes of silent apprehension, during which Goodhare's savage droning went on again, Deborah felt sufficiently secure to indulge the overwhelming anxiety and curiosity which prompted her to look at him in his den and discover whether he was really alone.

She crept over the floor, cautiously feeling with her feet before every step she took, and reaching the half-open door, found it easy to peep into the lower cellar without being seen by Goodhare. For he was sitting on the opposite side of the square grate, leaning on his elbow along one of the wooden benches, with a great pewter tankard beside him and two or three empty bottles at his feet. He was reaching the sleepy stage of intoxication, she thought, for his face wore an expression of dull ferocity as he stared into the fire.

Suddenly he lifted his head and assumed a listening attitude, becoming on the instant alert and fierce. Deborah withdrew at once from the door, afraid that he had seen her. But the next moment she heard sounds on the floor above, and a step which she thought was Rees Pennant's. Creeping back to the wall she listened intently, and heard Goodhare push the door of the inner cellar wide open, just as some one began to climb down the ladder.

"Rees!" whispered Amos rather huskily.

"All right."

They disappeared together into the lower cellar, pulled the door after him, and drew the bolt.

Deborah crept close to the small nail-holes where once a lock had been fixed, hoping to learn what had become of Lord St. Austell, about whom she felt every minute more anxious. She could see nothing through the holes but the glow and flicker of the fire on the walls, but she was able to distinguish every word of the conversation.

"Well," Rees began, in a spiritless and surly voice, "you seem to have been enjoying yourself."

"I have," assented the other, in a tone of such savage satisfaction that Deborah seemed to feel the blood grow suddenly cold in her veins. "There's nothing else to be done till Sep comes back."

"He has come back," said Rees shortly.

"Come back!" echoed Goodhare in a tone of anger and consternation. "What the d—l has he come back for?"

"You'd better ask him. I met him just now standing shivering and hesitating at the outer door of our room."

"But he never went then! He can't have been to Amsterdam and back since yesterday!"

"I should say not."

"Then what has the fool done with the jewels?" asked Amos, whose tones grew more furious every moment.

Already he had drawn the bolt of the door.

"From what I could make out, some woman's got them. But the poor wretch was in such an abject state of funk that I couldn't get much that was intelligible out of him."

Goodhare stammered out an oath. He seemed to be choking with rage as he burst opened the door with a rough hand.

"A woman!" he growled out. "I'll tear the heart out of her."

"If you can get hold of her," says Rees drily. "But as I thought you'd make things unpleasant for the poor chap, I pushed him out of the front door and told him to put a couple of miles between you and him as fast as possible."

Goodhare turned, very slowly. The shock of this intelligence, imparted thus coolly, seemed for the moment to overwhelm him. Then, with a howl of rage, he sprang at Rees, who nimbly avoided him.

"You dare to defy me, to help this miserable cur to escape me!"

"Yes, I tell you I'm sick of the whole business, this dog's life and all. And I'm not sorry the jewels are gone, that I can be quit of knavery and you together. You seem to be pretty well 'on' to-night, and in you're true colors you're by no means fascinating."

Goodhare seemed, however, to perceive the need of pulling himself together. There was a short pause before he answered, in a quieter tone:

"Don't you think you're rather ungrateful? You must own that I've shown you how to enjoy yourself, and given you the means to do it, too."

"A poor sort of enjoyment! I'm the wreck of what I was a year and a half ago!"

"Only shows how alluring you found pleasure, that you gave yourself up to it so completely."

"Well, I've had enough of it now. I'm going back to Carstow, where I've left a good little girl dying for love of me. I'm going to settle down to quiet respectability and forget that I ever saw your cursed face."

"And on what money do you propose to do this?"

"That's my affair."

"No; mine."

Rees had miscalculated the old man's activity, as well as his patience. Having been in the habit of treating Goodhare with impertinence, which the ex-librarian always bore without protest, the short-sighted and vain young man thought he need set no bounds to his pertness. But as a matter of fact, every insult, every slight which he had ever put upon his accomplished tutor in evil-doing, had been stored up in the mind of the latter, who only waited to destroy his tool until he should have no further need for it. That time he thought had now come.

Maddened by the shedding of blood—that last crime which he had tried within the past hour—Goodhare gave rein to the demoniacal side of his nature, and showed all the hatred and contempt, which had been gathering in his mind against the young man since their connection first began, in one look, one exclamation which turned the young man's blood cold, even before he felt the sinewy grip of the lean fingers about his throat.

"I'll serve you," he growled, "as I've just served a better man." And, drawing from one of his pockets the same knife with which he had stabbed Lord St. Austell, he made a dash at Rees Pennant's breast. But the young man was more alert than the old one had been. He flung out his hands, struck, struggled, and writhed to such good purpose that his assailant could not despatch him with the neatness he had shown in his attack on the earl. It was not until the third stab that Rees fell back with a groan, and slipping from Goodhare's murderous hands, sank on to the nearest bench, and thence in a heap on to the floor.

The sight of the young fellow's body, and the red stain that was spreading on the matting at his feet, seemed to sober Goodhare and bring him for the first time to a knowledge of his position. He glanced at the door, for he thought he heard sounds outside. Then, kneeling hastily down by Rees Pennant's motionless body, he ransacked all the pockets of the young man's clothes with eager, swift fingers. He had fancied that in them he should find the jewels, believing that Rees had either gone shares with Sep in them, or appropriated them all, with the idea that such audacity would never be suspected. Finding no trace of either jewels or money, beyond a handful of loose silver, Goodhare started to his feet, for the first time utterly horror-struck and confounded. Had he really lost his best chance of recovering the jewels? For Rees Pennant's influence over Sep was infinitely greater than his own; besides, the story of Sep's escape might be true.

With real solicitude he stooped over the silent huddled-up figure on the floor.

"Rees, Rees, old boy!" he cried, in a voice full of anxiety.

But he got no answer.

Enraged beyond measure, and still too much excited to be quite master of himself, he gave the inanimate body an impatient kick, and rising hastily, drank the remains of a bottle of wine without taking the trouble to pour it into the tankard, climbed out of the room, and up the ladder on to the ground floor.

Here, however, he came to a sudden check. Somebody had begun to hammer violently at the back door and just as he was making for the front, resolved to try to burst it open, he heard the sound of somebody battering it from the outside.

A moment's thought showed him the only course open. Just as he heard the sound of the first board giving way under the crashing blows which were being hailed upon it, he sprang up the rickety stairs.

CHAPTER XXIV.

As soon as the altercation between Goodhare and Rees grew warm, Deborah, hearing the tramp of footsteps on the pavement outside the house, had crept to the cellar window, and, unheard by the two men in their excited discussion, had torn away one of the boards from the nail which fastened it, and succeeded in attracting the attention of a passer-by, who proved to be policeman.

"Get in! break in! get in somehow!" she cried, "there are two men quarrelling here, and I'm afraid they will do each other harm."

By that time the voices in the lower cellar were growing louder, and she stumbled across the floor, called to the men, and beat against the door. But they were too much excited to heed her. She heard upstairs the sound of knocking; and climbing up the ladder as fast as she could in the darkness, she groped her way to the front door. There was, however, nothing that she could do to help. She could only wait, sick with terror, while they hammered in the nailed-up door from the outside. Before the first board gave way, she heard someone pass her in the darkness and spring up the staircase. From the agility with which he mounted she thought it must be Rees.

"Rees, is it you? Are you safe? Hide, hide yourself," she called to him in a hissing whisper.

Amos Goodhare heard her voice and recognised it. It flashed through his mind instantly that it must have been to her that Sep had given the jewels. If he could only get possession of them, the day's work which had rid him of a troublesome confederate and satisfied his appetite for revenge on two men he hated, would be indeed well done.

He descended the stairs as softly and rapidly as he had mounted them.

"Yes, Deborah, it is I, Rees," he said, in a whisper which was only just audible in the noise of knocking, both at the front and the back of the house. "Where are you? Give me your hand. You have the jewels?"

"Yes," she answered, hesitatingly.

"Where are you? where are you?" he repeated impatiently. "Quick; I must be off."

But he had betrayed himself. Deborah, shocked, alarmed, crept along the wall away from him, uttering no sound. He groped about for her, muttering to himself, until, with a crash, one of the boards of the door fell. By the light which was thus let in, he saw where the girl was, and sprang at her. But she pushed him off with a piercing shriek, avoided nimbly a second attack, and got back to the front door just as it was quivering on its hinges. Goodhare saw that he had no more time to lose.

"Good-bye, my dear; my love to Rees," he said, as he re-mounted the staircase rapidly, and disappeared from view just as the front-door fell down with a crash on to the rotten flooring, and four policemen rushed in.

"Upstairs, upstairs, he's escaped upstairs," panted out Deborah.

Two out of the four men mounted the staircase in pursuit; the other two remained with her and wanted to know what had happened.

"I don't know myself yet," she answered. She was still breathless and trembling from her recent encounter with Goodhare, and feverish with anxiety on Rees Pennant's account.

The officers seemed inclined to look upon her with suspicion. Deborah noticed this, and tried hard to compose herself.

"I want you to go downstairs—into the cellars," she cried. "They were quarreling there, and one of them ran upstairs past me while I was standing here."

"And what might you be doing here, miss?" asked one of the men, not uncivilly, but in a tone of cautious inquiry, which woke Deborah suddenly to a full knowledge of the dangerous thing she was doing in letting the servants of the law into this busy little nest of villainy. She had thought only of summoning help for Rees when she fancied that he was physically at the mercy of a savage and unscrupulous man; now she saw that by so doing she had perhaps betrayed Rees into the clutches of the law.

There was no help for it now, however.

"My name is Deborah Audaer," said she. "I live at Carstow, in Monmouthshire. I will give you any particulars you want later."

"What was it you said about the cellars, miss?" asked the other constable, as the lady paused.

Deborah turned desperately towards the ladder.

"This way down," said she briefly, as she led the way herself.

It was quite dark, and the constables were unprovided with any light except matches, which they struck from time to time as they blundered down. It occurred to her that if Rees were unharmed and had failed to take warning by the noise of the policemen's forcible entrance, she might find a chance of aiding his escape. So she hurried down as fast as she could, and stood with her back to the door of the lower cellar, so as to hide the fire-light which showed through the hole made by the old lock.

"Search this place first, please," said she.

"I'll light my lantern," said one of the men.

The other struck a match, and examined the den as well as he could by its feeble light.

"What's that in the corner?" said the first man.

Deborah was not paying much heed to their discoveries. She was watching for an opportunity, when their backs were turned, of slipping down into the adjoining cellar to find out what had become of Rees. But an exclamation from both men at once, as they crossed with their heavy tread to the corner indicated, riveted her attention.

"Look here, miss," called one of them.

Deborah crept forward, prepared for some horrible sight, and thinking still of Rees.

On the damp, muddy floor, with a piece of old and frayed matting wrapped around it, lay the body of a man. As Deborah drew near, the flickering match held by the policeman went out, and while he struck another his companion laid his hand on the lady's arm with evident suspicion. Deborah did not resent the touch; she stood in a dumb agony of dread.

When the lantern was lighted, she dared not look; the policeman drew her forward.

"Will you besergood as to tell us whether you know the gentleman?"

She glanced down, and utterly unable to restrain herself, almost shrieked:

"Lord St. Austell! Dead! Murdered!"

The men looked at each other and at her. By her tone they knew that the sight was for her a ghastly surprise, and the man who had held her arm at once let it go. Lord St. Austell was a well-known and popular peer, and, looking closer, one of the policemen recognised his face.

"She's right. The lady's right, Bill," said he more respectfully.

And the men looked at each other and at Deborah again. The dead earl's character was so well-known that their first thought was of an ambush laid, with a handsome woman as decoy.

"Do you know who's done this, ma'am?" asked one, bluntly.

"Yes, the man who escaped upstairs; his name is Amos Goodhare," she answered promptly. "But come into the inner cellar. There may be another murdered man lying there," she cried, rousing herself suddenly out of the numb apathy into which the horrible sight had cast her.

"You go, Fred; I'll stay here."

The other nodded and accompanied her to the door of the inner cellar, where Deborah fumbled for a minute with weak, wet fingers.

"Open it," said she hoarsely.

The man did so, and leapt down at once into the den. The fire was getting low now, but the air was still as hot as a furnace, and there was enough light for him to find his way to the prostrate form of Rees.

"By Jove! Another!" he muttered.

Deborah got down with difficulty, and tottered with swimming brain across the floor.

"Rees, Rees!" she whispered. "Dead, too!"

"No, miss, not quite—this one," said the policeman, trying to speak re-assuringly, but growing every moment more perplexed by the whole affair. "This poor chap may come round, I think, if he ain't bled too much. Let's try to stop the bleeding if we can."

Scarcely knowing what she did, Deborah lent her aid. Pressing her fingers to the wound, she said imploringly:

"Go and fetch a doctor as quickly as you can, please. It is his only chance."

"All right, miss," said the man.

And, quite satisfied that she would not move from the side of the handsome young fellow, he went out at once. Although, in the close, stifling atmosphere of the cellar, absorbed in grief and anxiety of the most bitter kind, Deborah fancied that she passed an hour kneeling by the side of the unconscious man, with her fingers tightly pressing together the sides of the ghastly wound in his chest, it was really not more than seven minutes before the policeman came back with a doctor.

"There's a gentleman just got into the house from the back, miss," said the constable. "He doesn't seem to know anything of what's been going on, and I haven't told him, but he asked if there was a lady here, and I told him there was."

"A gentleman!" echoed Deborah, as she rose from the floor, and staggered, overcome by the stifling heat.

She glanced down at Rees. He was in the doctor's hands now; she could do no more for him. She was glad to escape out of this horrible den, and she climbed up the ladder to the ground floor without further question. A short, fair man, with a strong sense of his own importance apparent in his face and bearing, but evidently suffering for the time from some deep anxiety, was waiting in the passage. He carried a lamp which Deborah had seen on the table at Rees Pennant's lodgings, and by its light she recognised the Honorable Charles Cenarth, keeper of the regalia.

"My niece, Marion, followed her father and you to a house in St. Martin's-lane, and then she drove to my house and brought me here. She was afraid of coming alone, lest he should be angry. And a young man who was hovering about outside showed me the way to this place——"

"Sep Jocelyn," murmured Deborah.

"And told me he thought my brother had come here. Perhaps you, Miss Audaer, can tell me where Lord St. Austell is."

Deborah paused. She had no fear of inflicting a very severe wound on this deliberate gentleman by informing him of his elder brother's death. It was pretty well known that the Honorable Charles looked upon the earl chiefly as the man who stood between him and the title.

"You are Lord St. Austell now," she said, gently.

He honored the announcement with a start of surprise, but made no show of being deeply affected. There was a pause.

"How was it?" he asked, trying to keep his hands out of the pockets to which they instinctively felt their way.

"He was murdered, I think, by Amos Goodhare," she answered in a whisper.

"Dear me, how very stupid of him to trust himself with Amos," said the new earl, fretfully. "Have they caught him yet?"

"Not yet, I think."

"Then I hope they won't! I hope to God they won't! It's an awkward position, don't you see? And the fellow does say such unpleasant things."

Deborah was disgusted. But she had something of importance to say to this phlegmatic gentleman, and it was perhaps fortunate in one way that he was unemotional.

"I have a favor to ask of you," she said.

He pricked up his ears. "A favor! It's of no use asking favors of me, Miss Audaer. I'm not my unfortunate brother, you know," he said hastily.

"You need not trouble yourself on that point. Nobody is likely to mistake you for him."

"So much the better. I'm a poor man. The estates are very heavily encumbered, owing to my unhappy brother's extravagance, his lamentable extravagance, I repeat. So that it is quite out of my power to grant favors—quite."

"Even when they put money into your pocket?" said Deborah, who thought he deserved this plain-speaking.

He was not in the least offended.

"Tell me what it is?" said he at once.

At that moment the noise of a scuffle and men's cries, "I've got you, my lad." "Hold him, Jim!" in the upper part of the house reached their ears.

"They've caught him!" cried Deborah, with excitement.

The new Lord Austell gave an exclamation of impatience.

"Well, well, tell me at once what you want, before we are interrupted."

Deborah had known how to gain the ear of the generous nobleman.

CHAPTER XXV.

THE new Earl of St. Austell was not the man to lose any opportunity of making a good bargain. Deborah Audaer had promised to ask him a favor which should put money in his pocket, and although he was puzzled by the offer, he was so desperately anxious to hear it that the news of the capture of his brother's supposed murderer came to him only as a tiresome interruption.

"Well, well, this favor you want of me, what is it?" he repeated, impatiently. "Of course, Miss Audaer, you know I am only too happy at any time to——"

"Thank you, yes, of course," answered Deborah, with one eye upon him and one upon the staircase, as the sounds of voices and scuffling seemed to subside a little. "I want to ask you if you will forgive any injuries you or poor Lord St. Austell may have received from two men who were merely the tools of Amos Goodhare. I can convince you that they had nothing to do with his murder; in fact, one of them has been stabbed by Amos so severely that I am afraid he may not recover. Will you promise this?" A pause, during which Charles Cenarth looked doubtfully at the candle. "I should not have had to ask your brother twice," she added, with a touch of dry irony.

"And where is the advantage this would bring to me?" asked he, doubtfully.

"I could restore to you the lost jewels. The setting I believe, is gone beyond recovery."

He looked at her as if he could scarcely believe his ears.

"Restore the jewels!" he repeated, hardly daring to utter the words aloud. Then he added with an abrupt change of tone: "If you know where they are you are bound to give them up."

"Yes, so I am—to the police," said Deborah, quietly.

He looked at her askance, with much mistrust. This was a disagreeably sharp young woman.

"Offenders against the law ought to be punished!" he said severely. "I am not the man to compound a felony."

"Then, your lordship, I am at liberty to make known whatever I have learnt to the police."

"And give up these people you are so anxious to shield?"

"No; persuade them to turn Queen's evidence."

He began to move about impatiently.

"Have it your own way, then, and for goodness sake let me know where the jewels are, and get this business over."

"You give me your word of honor that you will not only refrain from taking proceedings against any man but the murderer, but you will help to shield the others from the effects of their own folly?"

"And wickedness," added the earl, severely.

"And wickedness."

"You are asking a great deal," said the new Lord St. Austell, with a wry face. "Do you know the reputation I bear?"

Deborah did. It was that of a close-fisted and sanctimonious prig.

"Well, your lordship, you have only to say no, and I will set about getting these unfortunate men out of their scrape in another way."

She turned away impatiently. The noise of a heavy tramp of feet was heard coming down the stairs. The new earl tapped her arm petulantly.

"I agree! I agree! I give my word of honor!" he mumbled, "And now get me the jewels as fast as you can," he continued, in a burst of eagerness.

Deborah brought out from under her cloak the two small flat paper parcels which Sep had given her, and placed them in the earl's hands. He tore one of them open and quickly examined the contents. By his little murmur, by his very attitude, she saw that she need have no further fear for Rees or Sep. Indeed, the recovery of the jewels meant for him, social salvation. He buttoned them up hastily under his coat, hugging as it were himself and them as he did so. He had not time to repent having got them back by a bargain instead of by cheaper strategy, when Amos Goodhare, secured at last, was forced down the stairs by his captors with no great gentleness, and brought face to face with the brother of the man he had murdered.

He had been seized by the policemen just as he was endeavoring to escape into the next house, by scrambling from window to window; he had got loose again, had squeezed through a trap-door on to the roof, and after a chase along the leads, rendered more exciting by their dangerously ruinous condition, he had been caught, dragged back, handcuffed, and finally brought down the staircase by which he had ascended.

"Who's this?" said one of the policemen roughly, as he looked the new earl up and down without apparently, having his suspicions allayed by any dignity in the little man's appearance.

"My brother," said Amos promptly.

"I am Charles Cenarth. It is my brother who has been murdered."

"Oh, ho! You don't acknowledge your relationship to me, then," said Goodhare in a mocking tone. "That's ungrateful, when I've done for you what you'd never have dared to do for yourself," he added, darting forward to whisper into the little man's unwilling ear.

"This gentleman is connected with my family and I'm sure he will be able to give a perfectly satisfactory account of himself," said his frightened kinsman nervously.

"Hope so, I'm sure," said one of the policemen drily.

"Could you not let him go?" suggested the new earl uneasily.

"No, sir; I'm afraid we couldn't see our way to it. Gentlemen found running away in a house where a murder has been committed isn't let off quite so easy."

"Murder! Who said there was a murder?"

The man pointed to the constable who had brought the doctor to Rees.

"This man and the young lady there found the body."

"The young lady," cried Goodhare mockingly. "The young lady's word isn't worth much. If you take her to the station and have her searched, you will find on her a quantity of jewels of great value, stolen from the Regalia at the Tower."

Evidently some rumor of the theft, quiet as the matter had been kept, had reached the ears of the force. For they looked at each other, and one of them stepped quickly forward, with his hand raised, towards Deborah. To her great surprise, the decorous Charles Cenarth came to the rescue with a deliberate and roundly uttered falsehood.

"I don't know what the prisoner hopes to gain by this ridiculous charge against a young lady," he said, gravely. "But as I happen to be Keeper of the Regalia, no one can prove better than I that she cannot be in possession of any of the crown jewels, as none of the crown jewels have ever been stolen."

"Ah, ah! Very good! Very good, indeed, brother Charles," said Goodhare, mockingly.

The police officers said nothing to all this. They began to "smell a rat," however; for if there had been nothing in the rumored theft, what should two such prodigious swells as the earl and his brother do poking about in this thieves' den, with such disastrous results for one of them? As there was nothing to be got by contradicting the "swell's" assertion, the man who had approached Deborah stepped back respectfully.

"Come on," said he to his companions, "we'll make sure of this one, anyhow."

And he looked at Goodhare, who had subsided into silence.

"There's another of 'em downstairs, ain't there?" asked one of the others.

"He's done for, I think."

But at that moment there came up from the cellar the doctor and the fourth policeman, supporting between them the weak and almost helpless

Rees Pennant, who tried feebly to walk, but was scarcely able to do more then drag his feet limply after him.

"This man had nothing to do with the murder," said Deborah hastily, glancing in fear towards Amos Goodhare as she laid her hand on one of Rees's helpless arms.

"No, that is right enough," said Goodhare at once, to Deborah's surprise. "He had nothing to do with it."

There was a malicious expression on the old scoundrel's face which did not accord with the words. The policemen, though not at all satisfied as to the share Rees Pennant and Deborah had taken in this mysterious affair, contented themselves with taking their names and the address at Carstow which the young lady gave them, on Charles Cenarth's offering to go to the police-station and to become security for their appearance when they should be wanted. For it was apparent to everyone that the young man's injuries were of a dangerous, if not fatal description.

On learning from the questions of the constables how important a factor her own evidence against Goodhare would be, poor Deborah could not suppress a little cry of horror. Strong as were her mistrust and dislike of the ex-librarian, the thought that it might be her words which would convict him was so terrible that, as he passed her on his way out, she gave him a look as if to implore his forgiveness.

Amos Goodhare, who, now that he was caught, was very quiet and subdued, stopped short with a low cry of pain as soon as the constables who had him in charge attempted to lead him forward.

"I am hurt," he said, in a low voice. "One of you infernal ruffians must have done it when you caught me, two men against one. Let the doctor see my ankle, my right ankle—I think I have sprained it."

With the constables' help he limped back to the bottom stair and sat down. While the men stood back to allow the doctor to examine the limb he declared to be injured, and Deborah reluctantly held the lamp, Amos looked up malevolently into her face.

"Don't apologise, Miss Audaer, for any injury your evidence might do me?" he said in a rapid whisper. "By giving you back your lover, Rees Pennant, now that I have done with him, I show you that I bear no malice."

"Thank you," said she quietly. "I appreciate your kindness."

"I hope you may find a young scoundrel more to your taste than an old one."

Deborah made no answer. The doctor having declared that there was no sign of a broken or displaced bone, and that the pain Amos spoke of must be the result of a slight sprain, he was helped on to his feet again, and led out of the house by his captors, followed by Charles Cenarth, who was to accompany them to the police station.

Deborah then asked the doctor if it would be safe to take Rees as far as Carstow that night. He answered with a decided negative. As she stood wondering what she should do with him, a hand was laid on her arm, and turning, she saw Lady Marion Cenarth, lean, haggard, despairing. She had crept into the house after her uncle, and remained in a distant corner, unseen in the darkness, unheard amid the general excitement.

"Bring him to my aunt's," she whispered imploringly. "Not Mrs. Charles Cenarth, but an aunt of my mother's. She would take charge of him, I know. And if I could be of any use in nursing him—" she added piteously, imploringly. "Do let me. Oh! do let me," she continued in a heart-broken tone. "Let him love you, and marry you—I don't care. Only don't take him quite away—until he is well."

Deborah was touched. She took the girl's hand and answered very gently:

"I don't want to take him away from you. I shall be very glad if your aunt will take him in for a little while."

So Rees was half-led, half-carried out of the house and along the little court, and lifted into a cab, in which he and Deborah and the faithful Marion were driven slowly as far as Hill street, where old Lady Susan Mortimer lived. As Lady Marion had prophesied, they were all made welcome by the little old lady, who was of a highly sentimental turn of mind, and took her grandniece's part heartily against the girl's more worldly-minded parents. She sent at once for her own doctor, and in the meantime had Rees carried into the best bed-room, a large and gloomy chamber, with a funereal four-post bedstead of carved wood, with hangings darkened by age.

When the young fellow had been laid carefully on this sombre couch, Deborah, who saw that he would have no lack of attention, attempted to retire from the bedside. But Rees, who had been lying with closed eyes, opened them suddenly to say:

"Where are you going, Deborah?"

"I'm going back to Carstow to tell mamma you are all right. She will be anxious."

He half raised himself feebly.

"Very well, then, I shall come with you," he whispered obstinately. "I'm not going to stay here without you."

"Nonsense, Rees. You mustn't be ungrateful. It would kill you to travel to-night."

In the meantime, poor, meek-spirited Lady Marion had begged her great-aunt to invite Deborah to stay.

"He wants her, you see," she added pitifully.

So little Lady Susan trotted forward and said that if Miss Audaer would stay and help to nurse Rees she should be very pleased. And Deborah, with some reluctance, had to yield.

CHAPTER XXVI.

DEBORAH was saved the pain of giving evidence against Amos Goodhare, for that gentleman, having by his ruse of a sprained ankle, put the policemen in whose charge he was a little off their guard, managed to escape from their guardianship before they got to the end of the court, and by means of the London fog which had helped him so much already, got away, doubled on his pursuers, and took refuge, with great astuteness, in the very house in which he had been caught, even before the men who were now in charge of the body of the murdered man had left the building with their burden.

Amos was never caught; indeed, the authorities seemed rather slack in his pursuit; and as he had the astuteness to leave the country immediately, nothing more was ever heard of him until two years later, when he died in Paris, in abject poverty.

The sensational death of Lord St. Austell was never fully explained to the public. As the recovered crown jewels were immediately re-set and restored to their places among the rest, the temporary loss of them was never widely known, and the country bumpkins who go to the Tower to stare at the treasures, which many Londoners have never seen, are still as much impressed as ever by the antiquity of the gold of King Edward's crown. So that the murder of the earl was generally believed to have been merely the sequel to a commonplace affair of robbery, affected by means of a decoy.

Rees and Sep also got off much more easily than they deserved, the whole affair having died out of the public mind before the former was in a fit condition to be moved from Lady Susan's house to his mother's home in Carstow. But Rees was injured for life. No physician could give him hopes of more than a sickly existence, with constant danger of the re-opening of the wound. So much his excesses of the past year had done to undermine a fine constitution. And another wound was in store for him.

Sep crawled back one cool April evening, shivering, miserable, and half crazy, from want on the one hand, and a guilty conscience on the other, to his old aunt at Carstow, who took him in and nursed and tended him with unquestioning goodness. But he was never the same man again. Without suffering evidently from impaired reason, he fell into a lethargic state, and was subject for the few remaining years of his life to fits of nervous depression which nothing could cure. One sign of the change in him was that he hated the sight of Rees, and would turn hurriedly out of his way as soon as his formerly beloved companion came in sight.

Rees, in spite of his wound, took things more easily, and was easily nursed back, by the adoration of his mother and of Lady Marion, into nearly his old belief in himself. Lady Marion, whose devotion was, if possible, more pronounced than ever, returned to Llancader as soon as he went back to Carstow, in order to be as near to him as possible. His evident preference for Deborah did not disconcert her; she was resigned to everything but losing sight of him, and accepted any small crumbs of gratitude and kindness which he chose to throw to her with humble joy.

Partly, perhaps, because Deborah showed no particular devotion, but more of a kindly and even contemptuous pity in her ministrations to his comfort, Rees showed for her something nearer to genuine affection than he had ever showed to a girl before. Nothing was done rightly for him except by her; and as Mrs. Pennant had not resolution enough to interfere with any caprice of her darling boy's, the young girl was in danger of losing her health by the close confinement his demands upon her care involved.

At last Godwin, whose disgust was unbounded at the fuss made over the returned prodigal, stepped in to say a necessary word for Deborah. Since his brother's arrival, Godwin had been on very distant terms with her, having given Rees a colder welcome than she thought right. They had, therefore, not held any conversation together except of the most formal kind, when, finding, an one of his fortnightly visits, that she began to look pale and dull-eyed, he ordered her out for a walk in such an angry and peremptory tone that his mother backed up his command with coaxing words of entreaty.

"Yes, dear, go, do go," said the old lady, who had now almost recovered from her paralytic stroke, but who had been, since that misfortune, more afraid of masculine wrath than ever. "Godwin is quite right. You do want a walk. Rees will let you go, I'm sure; he's never selfish."

The poor old lady really believed this; and Godwin's grunt on hearing her ingenuous remark was not likely to undeceive her.

Rees, who was still confined a great deal to the house, gave an unwilling consent to Deborah's going out "for an hour."

"Only for an hour, mind," he added, as she went out of the room. "I shan't drink my tea unless you make it. I don't want to be poisoned."

"All right, Rees, only an hour," sang out Deborah good-humoredly, as Godwin closed the door for her.

As soon as he had done so, Godwin walked over abruptly to the armchair in which Rees was leaning back.

"Do you know that you ought to be ashamed of yourself not to give more thought to that girl's comfort?" he said, in what both Rees and his mother considered a cruelly sharp tone. "How is she to keep her health if she is stuck in the house all day attending to your fads?"

155

"Godwin, Godwin," remonstrated Mrs. Pennant, shocked beyond measure at this irreverent treatment of her divinity, "you must not speak like that to our dear Rees! He knows there is nothing we would not, any of us, gladly do to help him to get well, and to wile away the tedious hours before he does get well."

"You don't quite seem to understand, Godwin, my boy," said Rees, with a touch of haughtiness, holding up his hand languidly to stop his mother. "I should be the last man in the world to take advantage of any girl's devotion to me. I am going to marry Deborah."

"Indeed! Well it's very good of you, I must say," said Godwin, with a bitterly ironical tone. "Of course, then, it's much easier for her to be a slave to your whims, since she knows it is to be for life!"

"Godwin, Godwin, my poor darling will be ill again if you speak so and excite him," wailed the mother.

"Serve him right. I never heard of such a pitiful sham martyr in my life," said Godwin, shortly; and not daring to trust himself to deliver such a lecture as he had in his mind, he went quickly out of the room, leaving Mrs. Pennant to sob on her darling's neck, and to assure him that he must forget every word of what his brother had so cruelly said.

"Remember, Rees dear," she went on tenderly, "he only speaks like that because he wanted to marry Deborah himself. But, of course, she preferred my own boy, my darling eldest son."

And she passed tremulous fingers through his curly hair.

"Have you told her yet that you mean to marry her?"

"Not yet, mother. I think I will to-night, after what that young cub said."

"Do, dearest. I suppose she knows what you mean to say to her; but she's been really very good and devoted to you, so why should you defer the pleasure it will give her?"

"All right, dear mother, I'll speak to her to-night—that is, if she's not too late to make my tea," he added, with the petulance of a spoilt child.

Meanwhile, Deborah, unmindful of the honor which was in store for her, was revelling in the fresh, sweet air of a spring afternoon. After a moment's debate as to where she should go, she turned her steps towards the river, crossed the bridge, and almost ran down to the meadow where, twenty months ago, the three confederates had found the second entrance to the underground passage.

She wandered along the river bank, looking now at the grey towers of the castle, and now at the pale green foliage which sparsely covered the trees on the opposite bank, when suddenly she was startled by two rapid steps behind her and a sharp touch, which was almost a light blow, on her shoulder.

Turning quickly, she saw Godwin, who looked angry and harassed. He stopped short, so she had to do the same.

"So you're to be my sister-in-law," he said, abruptly.

"Well?" said Deborah, quietly.

"I wish you joy of your post as wife to such a man as Rees has become."

"Is that kind of you?"

"I can't help it. I must say what I think for once. I'll never mention the subject again. If you like to be the slave of a man who hasn't it in him to care for you, what right have I to object?"

"What right, indeed," said Deborah.

"There, that's enough. I didn't know whether you, being a woman, could understand what a wreck, morally even more than physically, that unfortunate lad has become. So I thought I ought to warn you. Of course, I find it is useless; I might have known it would be."

"It is indeed," said she, in a peculiar tone.

"Of course, you think I am speaking from a selfish motive. But I am not. I gave up all hopes of you as soon as I knew that Rees was coming back."

"And devoted your attentions to the second Miss Brownlow?" asked Deborah, rather archly.

"No, that was all nonsense. I never spoke to the girl in my life, except to offer her a cup of tea," said Godwin, despondently.

"Didn't you?" asked Deborah slowly.

"No. Unlucky beggar that I am, I never can look at any other woman but you, except to find fault with her. I suppose it will be different when you are married. I hope so."

"And I hope not," said Deborah, laughing gaily.

Godwin looked at her with a rather puzzled expression.

"Don't you remember telling me," said she, saucily, "that a woman was always sorry to lose an admirer? How much more must this be the case, then, when that admirer is her own husband!"

Godwin stared at her in bewilderment. Deborah looked across at the castle.

"What on earth *do* you mean?" asked he, at last, slowly.

"Find out," she answered, making the words come in to a tune she was humming.

"Aren't you going to marry Rees?" asked he, in a loud and stolid tone.

"Not if he were an emperor or an angel," answered she, simply.

Godwin looked at her for a few moments as if he scarcely dared to take in the meaning of the situation.

"Then you'll have to marry me," said he decidedly.

"'Yes, if you please, kind sir, she said,'" answered Deborah, with a smile and a deep curtsey.

"But you don't love me," whispered Godwin, whose voice had suddenly broken and grown husky.

"Not more than I have done for the last six months. But then that's a good deal," added Deborah below her breath.

Rees Pennant displayed the rage of a spoilt child thwarted when, on the return of Godwin and Deborah together, the former announced their engagement. He stormed all that evening at the fickleness and insincerity of women, to a sympathetic accompaniment from his mother, who never quite forgave Deborah for what she called "jilting poor Rees."

Still in a tumult of angry pique, Rees straightway proposed next day to Lady Marion Cenarth, who accepted him with rapture. He duly married her before many weeks were over, in spite of the opposition of her relations. It was a fate much too good for him, but his punishment lay in the fact that he never understood this, but really believed that the abject sort of happiness Lady Marion found in ministering to his lightest caprice was a more than ample recompense for any woman's devotion.

Godwin, whose services by this time had proved valuable, was, within a few months of his marriage to Deborah, removed to Carstow, to take charge of the large estates in that neighborhood, where they both continued to lead the quiet life they liked best.

And so a second romance, of a brighter cast than the first, was ended in the shadow of the old grey castle walls.